The Overcomers

With bonus story:

More Precious than a Sunset

Two Christian Tales of Family, Fortitude and Faith

Phil Emmert

~~~~~

The Overcomers
A Book with Verve by *thewordverve inc.*

Cover design by Robin Krauss
http://www.bookformatters.com

Paperback interior and eBook formatting by Bob Houston
http://facebook.com/eBookFormatting/info
~~~~~

The Overcomers

Prologue

To him who overcomes, I will give the right to eat from the tree of life, which is in the paradise of God. (Revelation 2:7)

From the time a doctor holds us upside down, slaps us on the bottom, and we come squalling into this world—cold, hungry, and naked—until we gasp our last breath, we are in the process of overcoming.

For some, there are physical obstacles to overcome. For others, there are spiritual barriers, and for a few more still, there are the demons within.

This story features a family—and others in their town—who faced obstacles, things that weighed on their hearts, and thoughts and actions to the point where they could not see beyond them...until they did.

Jake Edmonds was obsessed with money and physical things that he did not have. He also held a caustic hostility against the man who killed his brother. Helen Dennis let men take advantage of her and abuse her. And she could not function without her alcohol fix. Marty, Maggie, and Jay just wanted love and attention. Perhaps we can learn through their stories how the love of God is able to conquer and bring passions into submission.

(1)

Jake Edmonds seemed like a nice enough young man to strangers and casual acquaintances. He appeared polite and pleasant, with an outgoing disposition. However, he showed a very different face to his wife and children.

Jake had married far too young, at only eighteen years of age. He had a large burden thrust upon him as his seventeen-year-old bride became pregnant in the first month of their marriage. That was June 1957.

He had rented a small upstairs apartment for them, which was hot in the summer and cold in the winter. But it was all he could afford. Eight years and two children later, they were still in that small four-room apartment.

Jake pumped gas and changed oil at an independent gas station owned by a friend of his father. He worked at least forty-eight hours a week for a dollar eighty-five an hour. In 1965, that was not a bad wage for such a menial job. By the time everything was taken out of his earnings, he brought home about seventy-five dollars a week.

Working with the public was interesting if not a little frustrating at times. The snobbish businessmen in their Cadillacs and Lincolns were a demanding lot.

The high school girls, driving flashy cars their daddies bought for them, flirted with him and tempted him at times. They would ask him to clean their windshield as they spread their legs apart and pulled their skirts much higher on their thighs than necessary.

Jake's wife was a stay-at-home mom. Martha, who everyone called Marty, didn't dress as well as the elegant country club ladies who came to the station; in fact, at first glance, one might have considered her a little dowdy in appearance. But she was actually quite lovely, and if enhanced by fancy clothes, makeup, and trips to the beauty salon, her beauty might have been more obvious. But this was not her life.

Sadly, Jake neglected Marty. He never complimented her, nor did he offer to dress her up. She had worn her auburn hair with its natural curl in exactly the same style since high school. Marty's last dressy outfit was three years old and had been purchased for her by her mother. However, despite Jake's shortcomings, Marty loved him dearly, and she was a good wife and mother.

Once in a while, Jake would load Marty and the kids into his rusty old Chevy and take them to the Dog-N-Suds drive-in for a hotdog and root beer. But mainly, Jake was sullen and petulant with his family. The two small children—Maggie, age seven, and Jay, age five—often grated on Jake's nerves in that tiny apartment. He would sometimes scold them after a long, hard day at the gas station. He didn't seem to understand they were only contending for his attention, and of course, simply acting their ages.

Now, Jake loved Marty and the children, but he felt defeated and didn't know how to show his love to them. He thought that money would solve most of his problems. He often contemplated, *If I just had more money, I would show them how much I love them.* He failed to understand that Marty and the children just wanted his attention and approval.

Marty never complained. She accepted her lot in life. Actually, Marty had been raised in a dysfunctional family. She had never known kindness from any man until she met Jake Edmonds.

Marty's mother, Helen Dennis, was a heavy

smoker and drinker, though fortunately, she was not a malicious drunk. To make up for her lack of attention, she'd actually spoiled Marty as a child by buying her things. However, these days, Marty seldom saw her mother. Jake didn't forbid Helen from visiting, but it was obvious he was not fond of Helen's drinking and did not appreciate her visits.

Marty's father had left the family when she was eleven years old, and she never saw him again. After that, a steady stream of men came to the house. They often drank and partied all night. Her mother told her they were her uncles. Of course, she knew better. Marty learned to hide from these men and lock herself in her room. They were always trying to touch her or kiss her when her mother was in a stupor.

When Marty met Jake, he was different. He was soft spoken and handsome, with thick, dark hair and a muscular build. His dark brown eyes were penetrating and seemed to take in every detail around him.

Jake was also a hard worker. He had gone to work at the gas station even before graduating from high school. He didn't smoke and only drank a beer occasionally. Marty found that refreshing.

They first met at a high school sock hop after a

basketball game. He was a senior, and she, a junior. Their dates consisted mostly of driving around and hanging out at the local drive-in. Jake didn't try to touch her like the men who came to her house. He didn't even kiss her until their second date.

Four months later, when this handsome young man asked Marty to marry him, she said yes right away. Marty caught Helen on one of her drunken binges and coerced her into signing the necessary "permission to marry" papers. She and Jake were married right after his graduation by a justice of the peace. Marty didn't go back to school her senior year.

Now eight years later, Jake and Marty both felt trapped. It seemed every time they tried to get out of that apartment and rent something better, there was an obstacle, with lack of money being the largest. They could never save enough to make the move. Jake doled out money to Marty a little at a time; she was given just enough to cover groceries and nothing extra for personal things. Every day Marty felt more like a housekeeper and nanny, except without compensation. She had no idea how much money Jake had at any one time. They had no savings or checking account. Jake paid the rent and utilities. What he had left over went into his pocket. There was normally only some change left at the end of the month.

Six days a week, Jake labored at that gas station, pumping gas, checking and changing oil, cleaning windshields, and airing up tires—all for people who looked down their noses at him.

Marty became more frustrated every day, trapped in an apartment with two small children.

On Sundays, they would occasionally take a ride in the country, and admire *other people's* houses and land. Then they would come back and fall asleep across their bed while listening to the radio, dreaming of a larger, nicer house. They didn't own a TV. They had an old used one when they first married, but it had stopped working, and Jake said they couldn't afford another one.

On very rare occasions, they would take the children to a Disney movie or a Western at the local drive-in. It was fifty cents for adults, and the children got in free.

Jake's parents, John and Edna Edmonds, were Christians who had overcome the tragedy of losing a child. Jake's brother was killed in an auto accident when Jake was just sixteen years old. He was five years older than Jake, who'd always looked to him as some kind of hero. Jake was still fighting with God over this loss.

John and Edna went to church twice on Sunday

and prayer meeting on Wednesday night. Several times, they'd tried to talk to Jake about church, but he pushed them away. Jake was not interested in *"their God."*

A time or two, Marty seemed interested. She occasionally let the Edmonds take the children to Sunday school with them. It gave her some time alone with Jake. But these times alone usually led to a spirited discussion about money or another place to live. These arguments often ended with Marty crying and Jake stomping out.

One Sunday morning, Marty accepted the invitation to go to Sunday school and church with John and Edna.

(2)

The County Line Church of Christ was a country church about five miles out of town. The building was ancient. Sunday school classes in the auditorium were divided by curtains, which were pulled to separate two classes. The attendees had to concentrate pretty hard to hear the teacher in that auditorium—it was loud with all the echoes and various conversations going on. This is where the older men and women attended Sunday school.

The young adults, teens, and small children attended classes in the basement of the church, where they used two garage doors to divide the area into three classrooms. The acoustics were slightly better there, but not much.

The old church was growing in numbers, as a new young preacher had been hired about six months before. The people were excited about the prospect of new members and an expanded evangelistic program.

When the worship service started that Sunday, Marty noted they had a piano, an organ, and a choir. The singing was loud and lively; actually, it was very good. Marty heard some songs that sounded familiar to her, but she had to keep her head buried in the hymnal because she didn't know all the words.

The preacher appeared to be about thirty years old, dressed in a suit that was a little too small for his muscular build. His wife was a pretty, blond lady with two children about the same age as Marty's children.

The preacher's wife sat right in front, her eyes never leaving her husband the whole time he preached. When they made eye contact, there was a wink or a smile exchanged between them. It made Marty feel really good to see how much love passed between these two people. She only wished she and Jake could have that kind of love.

Marty did not remember much about the message that morning. But as she sat there, a peace came over her that she had never felt before in her life. When she shook hands with the preacher and his wife at the door, they introduced themselves. He told her if she wanted to talk about anything, she was welcome to call, and he wrote his telephone number on her bulletin. His name was Larry Lawrence, and his wife's name was Louise. Everyone called her Lou.

When Marty started to address him as Reverend, Larry held up his hands and stopped her. "No, please just call me Larry or Brother Lawrence." Both Larry and Lou gave Marty a feeling of comfort. They exuded faith and stability. Whatever they had, she thought, *that's what I want.*

(3)

All that week, Marty could not get the morning service and the Lawrences out of her mind. She could hardly wait to go back. But when she spoke to Jake about the church, he became very quiet at first, and then finally in a loud voice, he told her to "shut the hell up about church!"

She turned her head away as tears streamed down her face. Jake had never used that kind of language with her before, even in their money discussions. She looked to see if the children had heard, but they were fussing over a toy that each claimed was theirs. Thankfully, they had not heard Jake's outburst.

The next Sunday, Marty asked Jake if he would like to go to church. He just looked at her with his penetrating eyes and shook his head. Marty could read him well and didn't press the matter. However, she and the children went with John and Edna once again to County Line Church.

Marty's Sunday school teacher was a middle-aged man by the name of Harold Reagan. He was well versed in the Bible, and it was obvious that he'd spent time studying the lesson. Harold made the people, places, and stories in the Bible come alive. Marty felt like she was actually in the middle of these wonderful Bible adventures.

That Sunday, the worship services meant more to Marty than the first time she'd come. She was intent on listening. The sermon was entitled "Majoring in Minors." It was about how society was majoring in unimportant, material, and temporary things, while ignoring the eternal things.

At one point, Larry paused and asked, "Where will you be one hundred years from now?" Marty was so used to living from payday to payday that she had never thought more than a week ahead. It was a provocative question.

When the invitation was given, Larry encouraged those who needed prayer, or to make a decision, to come forward. Marty so wanted to go forward for prayer, but she could not let go of the pew in front of her. It was as if her fingers were glued to the back of that pew.

All that week, she kept thinking about the preacher's question, *"Where will you be one hundred years from now?"* It haunted her. She had no idea where she would be five years from now.

However, that week, Marty began to do something she had not done since the first few months of her marriage. She awoke early and prepared Jake's lunch box and a nice breakfast. She sat down, drank a cup of coffee with him, and tried to make small talk. The conversation was one sided. He only grunted and had that sullen, gloomy look on his face.

As Jake started out the door, Marty stood in front of him, reached up, hugged his neck, and planted a kiss on his lips. He looked a little surprised, but he responded by kissing her back.

She said, "Have a nice day, babe."

He just grunted back, "Okay," and rushed down the stairs.

Marty did something else too. She went into the bedroom and opened her hope chest, which sat at the foot of the bed. It had been months since she had opened that old cedar chest. Rummaging through it, she found a Gideon Bible that her mother had probably lifted from a motel several years ago and had put in the chest. The book had never been opened that she knew of. It had the sweet scent of cedar on it. Some of the pages were still stuck together. However, she didn't read from it that morning. She just held it in her hands like one would hold a valuable treasure.

Then Marty closed her eyes and began to speak to God. She didn't repeat any prayer she had ever heard . . . because she didn't know any. But she asked God to bless her and her family. She confessed that she was a sinner. She thanked God for her children and for Jake. Then she said, "God, I am sorry I don't know how to pray." That was it . . . that was all she prayed, but it was a start. She was sure God hadn't heard her, because, in her mind, she didn't deserve for God to listen to her.

The week went much better for Marty. The children's behavior seemed so much improved. She rewarded their good conduct by taking them to the park. The three of them swung on the swings. The children went round and round on the merry-go-round, went up and down on the teeter-totter, and slid down the slides. They laughed as they walked, ran, and skipped back home. Then Marty let them help her make a batch of peanut butter cookies.

Come Sunday, Marty decided she would use a different tactic with Jake. She simply laid out Jake's nicer casual slacks, along with a blue shirt and a sports coat that he had not worn in months. She then asked him in a non-threatening way if he would like to go to church with her and the children.

Jake frowned, then sighed and said, "No, not today. I need to rest."

Marty didn't argue. She had done all she could do. The rest would be up to him.

Once again, the Sunday school class was interesting and even a little fun as the class did some role playing . It was about witnessing to those who are in an unsaved condition. Marty learned a lot that morning.

She learned that she actually was not in a saved condition herself. It was something she had never considered before. She knew she was a sinner, but she also knew she was basically a good person. Surely, God would let her in His heaven.

It was a sobering moment to realize that just going to Sunday school and church does not make someone a Christian or give him a free pass into heaven. She shook her head. *I need to think about this some more. I can't wrap my mind around this right now.*

Marty realized that Communion had been served each Sunday she had been to church. The Edmonds

had informed her that it was offered every Sunday —
for those who were Christians.

Even though Marty didn't partake, she was
observant in this special time of the service, which
seemed so important to the congregation. There were
one or two people who wept openly during this
service. Some she noticed were moving their lips
with their eyes closed, as if silently talking to
someone. Even though she did not participate, it was
a moving experience for her. These people were
communing with Jesus Christ. She thought, *How
great that must be.*

The message this Lord's Day was entitled,
"Hated for Doing Good."

The preacher said this was the legacy of Jesus,
who was "hated for doing good." Jesus had healed
the sick, made the blind to see, restored hearing to
those who were deaf, and made the lame to walk.
Why, he had even cast out demons!

The preacher pointed out the straw that broke
the camel's back: Jesus had raised a friend of his back
to life after this man had been dead for four days.
The man's name was Lazarus. And because had
raised Lazarus back to life, his enemies set out to kill
Jesus.

Now Marty had never heard anything like this

before in her life. But she could see it unfold in her mind's eye. And the message stuck in her mind. *Hated for doing good.* The preacher had noted that followers of Jesus would also be hated for doing good. Marty wanted to follow Jesus, but she was conflicted; she didn't want to be hated. She thought, *No one wants to be hated.*

All that week, Marty arose early and prepared a nice breakfast for Jake that consisted of bacon, scrambled eggs, grits, and toast. She also made his lunch and put it in his lunch box. Sometimes, she would slip in a little note that said, "I love you" or "Hope you are having a good day."

Every morning as Jake was walking out the door, he was met with a smile, a hug, and a kiss from Marty. She was trying her best to go about *doing good.*

Satan loves to attack the weak and those who go about doing good. He worked on both Marty and Jake that week. Jake was vulnerable to Satan's attack. He remained serious, sullen, and quiet at home. But Marty was ready to go back to church. She wanted desperately to hear more.

It is sometimes strange how messages will stick in a person's mind. Marty could not get the last two messages out of her head: "Majoring in Minors" and "Hated for Doing Good."

She was bound and determined that she would get her husband to church by going around doing good for him. So she continued to prepare his breakfast and lunch. And every morning, Jake found her at the front door with a hug and a kiss, along with a wish for him to have a good day.

(5)

Satan planted a seed and began to work on Jake's mind. Jake began to suspect that Marty was fooling around since she was being so helpful and kind, sending those little notes. Satan will do that to a man.

You see, Marty had never actually done anything like this for Jake before. So on Wednesday of that third week, Jake did something which was not in his routine. He put a "Closed from 1 to 2" sign on the gas station door and went home to see what was going on. If Marty was fooling around, he would catch her.

Half a block from home, he shut the engine off on his old Chevy and coasted to the curb at their apartment. Creeping up the stairs, he quietly opened the door and slipped into the front room. *Way too quiet,* he thought. He glanced in the bedroom; no one was there. Looking into the children's room, he saw they were taking a nap. Tiptoeing toward the kitchen, he heard a voice. It was Marty. She was talking to someone.

Peeping around the door, he expected to see Marty and a man. Instead, Jake saw his wife sitting at the table with a book in her hands: a Bible. She had her head bowed and her eyes closed and she was speaking.

". . . and God, please bless my children. May Jake and I be able to raise them properly. Lord, may they do better in life than we have done. Lord, please bless Jake and keep him safe at work. I love him so very much . . ."

That was all Jake heard as he slowly backed out of the kitchen doorway and quietly closed the front door behind him.

Jake had never been an emotional man, but he had a lump in his throat as he started the old Chevy and pulled away. He also had a big dose of guilt in his heart for suspecting his wife of fooling around.

Little did Jake know that Marty was indeed trying to start a relationship—with Jesus Christ. Marty had been made aware that Jesus loved her even before she could ever love him.

***

Every day after lunchtime, when the children were down for their nap, Marty had a private session with Jesus. As the days grew into weeks, these sessions grew longer. She began to read the Bible and talk to Jesus sometimes for almost an hour at a time.

When school started, Maggie went into second grade and Jay started kindergarten. It was a little more difficult for Marty to get up early, fix three lunches, make sure everyone had a good breakfast before the school bus arrived, and see Jake off to work. However, almost every day she was able to accomplish this. If Jake noticed or appreciated Marty's efforts, he never said anything.

This hurt Marty a little, but she kept right on doing these things. It was her way of going about *doing good.*

Every Sunday, Marty had herself and the children scrubbed and dressed, then waited for John and Edna to come around and pick them up.

And every Sunday, she laid out Jake's clothes and asked him if he would like to come along. He always frowned and said, "Not today." He would usually give a feeble excuse, even though Marty never asked him for one.

One Sunday, as they were waiting for the Edmonds to arrive, little Jay looked up at his dad, took his hand, and asked, "Daddy, why don't you ever come to church with us?"

Jake was somewhat taken back by the question. He replied, "Maybe someday I will, Jay, but not today." His tone held no anger or frustration, as it had so many times before when asked about attending church.

(6)

One Sunday in November, Edna called and said that John was sick; they would not be able to pick up Marty and the children for church that day. Marty's heart sank, for she so looked forward to Sunday school and church. After she hung up, she turned to Jake and told him his dad was sick.

Could you take us to church today?" she asked, hesitant but hopeful.

Jake thought a minute with a frown on his face, and she prepared herself for a negative response. But he surprised her. "Okay," he said. Her face lit up until he added, "But I'll just sit in the car."

Marty said, "But that will be two hours, Jake."

"Well, I'll just come back and get you then."

Jake dropped the family off at the front entrance. One of the deacons, Dick Nelson, waved to Jake and asked him to come on in. Jake just waved back and said, "I can't today. Maybe some time, but not today."

For two hours, Jake drove around town. There was little activity; church parking lots were full, but there were no businesses open. He noted especially the Cadillacs and Lincolns in the parking lot of the large Methodist church uptown.

Just after noontime, Jake was back at County Line Church, waiting for his family. Soon, people started coming out, but they just congregated outside the front door, talking with each other. Several of them spied Jake and waved. A few of them were his regular customers at the gas station.

Finally, he saw Marty, Maggie, and Jay exit the church doors, smiling broadly. The children had crafts they had made and were showing them to the people milling around. Jake could not help but notice that the people were very friendly to his children. One man was passing out gum to all the kids. Jake thought he could never remember Christians being that friendly to him when he was little.

When Marty and the kids got in the car, Jake had a sudden thought. He turned around slightly in his seat and asked, "Who wants to go to the Dog-N-Suds?"

Three happy voices all shouted in unison, "Me!"

And so they had an elegant Sunday lunch at the Dog-N-Suds.

Jake knew it was not exactly how Marty wanted the Sunday to go—she would much rather all four of them had attended the services together—but it was a great day nonetheless. Jake was in cheerful mood. Not only that, a hot dog and root beer had never tasted better.

He could not forget the picture of his children smiling, showing off their crafts, and accepting the chewing gum from one of the men at church. It made him smile too. *That was really nice the way the people made over my children,* he thought. He loved his children dearly, and he wanted them to be happy.

(7)

When Marty came out of the bathroom that next Sunday morning, she was more than a little surprised to find Jake buttoning up the shirt she had laid out on the bed for him.

"Call Mom and Dad and tell them you have a way to church this morning," he said.

Marty quickly went to Jake and planted a huge kiss on his lips. Then she rushed to the phone and gave the Edmonds a call. The children almost burst with excitement when they saw that their daddy was going to church with them. Maggie and Jay chatted and giggled all the way to County Line Church.

Jake's parents were waiting at the front door of the church. His mom hugged him. His dad smiled from ear to ear and slapped Jake on the back.

Once in the classroom, Marty introduced Jake to the teacher, Harold Reagan. Harold grinned broadly and shook hands with Jake.

"No introduction is necessary," Harold said. "This fine young man pumps my gas and keeps my car running tip-top."

Jake said, "I had no idea you were the Sunday school teacher Marty keeps talking about."

As the class started, Harold introduced Jake to the five other couples in the class. Jake was a little surprised to discover that he actually knew some of them by first name already—they came into the station regularly. Immediately, he felt more at ease with these people, who were all within five or six years of his and Marty's ages.

Jake found the class just as interesting as Marty said it was. Harold wove wit and wisdom into his classes. Scripture was often quoted, and he gave his class members time to turn to the scripture and read it for themselves.

Marty shared her Gideon Bible with Jake. He let Marty turn to the scriptures; he felt a little embarrassed because he could not have found the passages as easily. He knew that Marty worked hard to memorize the books of the Bible so she could find the scriptures quickly. It was obviously paying off for her, and Jake knew she felt proud of herself. She had the New Testament books all memorized. He was proud of her too.

During worship, Jake, Marty, and his parents all sat in one pew together. The preacher remarked about how good it was to see all the Edmonds family sitting together.

When the offering was taken, Jake put a dollar in the plate and felt really generous. Marty smiled at him; she had never had any money to put in the plate before.

Larry Lawrence was in good form that day. He got the attention of the people with a funny preacher story. And then he got serious. The message was entitled, "He Who Overcomes," and it drew from the book of Revelation. Jake knew just enough about the Bible to know that was the last book. Larry pointed out that Jesus told each of the seven churches of Asia that they must overcome.

As Jake took in the message, he felt himself relating to it somewhat, for he had so many things he had to overcome if he was to be successful. He really wanted to get out of that cramped apartment. The children needed to have a yard to play in and a dog to romp with. But he felt hopeless. How could he overcome his problems? He had a hard time believing Larry, and the Bible. Overcoming was for people with money, houses, and land.

Jake left the church building feeling worse than

when he went in. He had missed the point of the message. His problem was not lack of money or physical things. He needed to overcome the devil. The devil was his adversary.

Several people greeted Jake after the service and invited him back. But as he listened to the people talk about the message, he thought, *They must not have heard the same message I heard.*

In the car, Marty also was bubbling over about how much the sermon meant to her.

It is amazing how two people can hear the same message and draw two different conclusions. Jake didn't know it, but Satan was sifting him. Satan was trying to separate him from the flock in order to attack and devour him.

(8)

Jake didn't go back to church that next Sunday—he found an excuse. The old car needed the oil changed. And so, Marty and the children caught a ride with the Edmonds while Jake changed the oil in his car.

When Marty got back home, Jake had just walked in the door, and he was angry. The car wasn't running right. It needed a new set of spark plugs.

Marty tried to make light of it and remarked, "Well, if you had gone to church this morning . . ."

That was as far as she got. Jake got in her face and shouted, "I don't want to hear that. I'll go to church when I damn well feel like it, and I'll stay home when I feel like it!"

Oh yes, Satan loves to attack the weakest lambs.

Marty began to cry. She had not meant to make him angry. She only wanted to make a point. As she cried, the children became upset. Jay ran to his mommy and got between Jake and her. Maggie ran to the bedroom.

There was no intimacy that week. But Marty still made the lunches and prepared the breakfast meals. She tried to hug and kiss Jake as he went out the door on Monday morning, but he stiffened and didn't return the favor.

***

All that week, it seemed that Jake was tempted at the station. The high school girls with their short skirts and even some of the country club ladies flirted with him. One man gave Jake too much money for gas, and Jake was tempted to put it in his pocket. But at the last minute, he returned the money and told the man about the mistake.

On Wednesday evening at closing time, one of Jake's high school buddies came in and invited him out for a beer. Jake gave in, and they went to the local pub. His friend bought a round. Then Jake bought a round. Another friend came in and ordered whiskey for all three of them. Jake tossed it down and chased it with yet another beer.

By the time he got home, he was pretty drunk. He was not used to drinking more than one beer at a time, and on an empty stomach at that.

The atmosphere was pretty tense that evening in the Edmonds home. Jake didn't want anything to eat, and he just went to the bedroom and fell into the bed.

Marty and the children ate by themselves in silence. Marty was so disappointed. She could not stand to live in another home where someone was drunk.

Before going to bed that night, Marty read her Bible. She read the scripture over in Revelation. She read every word that Jesus said to the seven churches of Asia. She marked the word "overcome" in each of the seven passages. She was bound and determined that no matter what Jake did, she would "overcome."

After praying for Jake and the children, and for her mother, she lay down very gently beside her husband and hugged him. Jake was out like a light and never felt that gentle hug.

Marty didn't change her routine. She was still going about doing good, just like a follower of Jesus should do.

***

By Saturday afternoon, Jake was feeling pretty guilty. The angry outburst, the temptation, the drunkenness . . . these were all playing on his mind. That evening after he closed the station, he pulled the car into an empty bay and changed the spark plugs.

(9)

Jake was the first one up on Sunday morning. After showering, he fixed French toast and bacon for everyone. By the time Marty came out of the bathroom, he was dressed for church. Together, they got the children ready. He called his parents and told them he would see them at church. He was going to give it another try.

The handshakes and the hugs lifted Jake's spirits some. He enjoyed the Sunday school class again. He even put two dollars in the offering plate. But as Larry got ready to speak, Jake was not really listening. He was thinking about all the bad things he had done this past week. He really wished there was some way to wipe the slate clean and start over.

The Holy Spirit works in strange ways. At the pulpit, Larry folded his sermon notes and put them in his coat pocket. He looked out at the congregation and, after a pause, he said, "I feel led to change my message this morning. But first, let's sing another song." He asked the ladies at the instruments to turn to the song "Whiter than Snow." He announced the hymn number and asked everyone to stand and sing.

The verse that stuck in Jake's mind was this one: *"Lord Jesus, I long to be perfectly whole, I want you forever to live in my soul, break down every idol, cast out every foe, now wash me and I shall be whiter than snow."*

After everyone was seated, Larry read Psalm 51:7 and began to preach with a passion that could only be the Holy Spirit speaking through his lips.

He quoted the Apostle Paul in Romans, who wrote of how we have all sinned and come short of the glory of God. Paul also wrote that the wages of sin is death, but the gift of God is life eternal through Jesus Christ. Then he said, "Put your name in that passage."

Larry went on to say our lives are like a blackboard with all our sins written on it. But the blood of Jesus Christ cleanses and erases all those sins if we apply that blood to our lives. He said, "We can start over fresh."

Jake thought, *Wow, Larry is reading my mind this morning.* He was touched by the message, but still was not ready to do anything. *Maybe someday, but not today.*

Satan tells us this all the time, *Someday, but not today.* If we keep saying this, Satan knows that one day it will be too late, and we will be with him in hell for eternity.

***

When the invitation was given, Marty motioned for Jake to let her out of the pew into the aisle. He didn't understand at first, but then she just pushed past him and walked very quickly to the front of the building just as the music stopped. She whispered to Larry that she wanted to accept Christ. She told him she had stood anchored to the floor through at least four or five invitations, and she could not stand through another one.

Marty made her confession of faith. "I believe that Jesus is the Christ, the Son of the living God." She was led by Lou and another lady to the dressing room where she donned a white baptismal robe, and then led to the steps of the baptistery, where Larry was waiting. They both stepped down into the water.

Larry said, "Martha Edmonds, because you have stated that you believe that Jesus is the Christ, the son of the living God, I now baptize you in the name of the Father, the Son, and the Holy Spirit. Amen."

The preacher dipped her beneath the water and lifted her back to her feet. Oh, such joy Marty had never felt in her life. The congregation with one voice said, "Amen." And they began to sing, *"Now I belong to Jesus, Jesus belongs to me, not for the years of time alone, but for eternity."*

It was a joyful time that day. Many people hugged Marty and wished her well. The elders and Larry then offered her communion after many of the people had already left. Still there were Jake, his parents, the children, and a dozen other people, who all witnessed as Marty partook of the Lord's Supper. It was even more meaningful to her than she anticipated. Such sweet communion with Jesus Christ.

(10)

Jesus said in Luke 15:10 that there is joy in the presence of the angels of God over one sinner that repents.

But the devil was very angry. And that week, Satan did his worst to make Marty sorry that she committed her life to Jesus.

He used Jake, the children, and even Marty's mother to make her sorry. Jake was very irritable with her that week. The children were fussy, and Jay's teacher called about him acting out in school. Maggie had a fever and needed to go to the doctor. Jake's mother was able to take Marty and Maggie for the appointment. But Jake was upset because the visit had cost ten dollars.

To top the week off, on Friday evening, Marty's mom, Helen Dennis, showed up at the house so drunk she almost fell coming up the stairs. Marty shut the door of the children's bedroom and brought Helen into the kitchen. She brewed a pot of coffee and poured her a cup. Helen was crying—her latest boyfriend had stolen money from her and had slapped her. Marty just listened without adding her own opinion.

Helen seemed somewhat surprised when Marty reached for her hand and held it between hers. She told Helen that she was going to pray for her.

It was not an eloquent prayer, but it was sincere and got to the heart of the matter. She asked God to take away her mother's desire to drink, and to give her mother the courage to tell all her male friends to get out of her house and never return. And finally, she asked God to forgive both her and Helen of their sins.

When Marty opened her eyes, her mother was staring at her with her mouth open in surprise and shock. Marty told her mother that she had accepted Christ as her Lord and savior. The news seemed to sober Helen, but she also seemed uncomfortable.

Marty asked her how she had gotten to her house today. "Surely you didn't try to drive?"

Helen said she had taken a cab. Marty poured her another cup of coffee and told her mother to go wash her face. If she would wait till Jake got home, she would give her some supper and see if Jake would take her home.

Her mother was hesitant, but eventually agreed to lie down on the couch for a while.

At fifteen past six, Jake walked in the door. A puzzled look crept over his face when he saw Helen asleep on the couch, the smell of booze obvious. He asked Marty what was going on. She filled him in and then asked him if he would take Helen home after supper. He made a face, but agreed.

That night, as Marty sat on the bed and brushed her hair, she thanked Jake for taking Helen home. He only grunted and sarcastically remarked that he was happy to do it . . . "to get her out of the house."

Marty ignored his sarcasm and said, "I am going to invite Mom to church on Sunday."

"Good luck with that," he said. "If she comes, I hope she doesn't embarrass us by coming drunk."

Marty didn't respond; she was on her knees beside the bed, praying.

(11)

The next few weeks went by rather quickly. There were good days and bad days. Just as the Apostle Peter had said in his letter, *"The devil is walking around seeking whom he may devour."* Marty claimed a promise that the Apostle John had made: *Greater is he who is in you, than he who is in the world.* She found an inner strength that she had never had before.

In the next two months, Marty and the children never missed a Sunday at County Line Church. Jake, however, was "hit and miss." Satan was really working on him.

As for Helen, she just laughed when Marty invited her to church. Still, Marty invited her every week.

At Christmas, the children were invited to participate in the church Christmas program. Maggie was just about the sweetest redheaded angel anyone ever saw. Jay practiced his part every day; he was a lamb in the stable. His part was to say, "Baa baa baa." Jay practiced a lot, and he got really good at it. He bleated at the table. He bleated when he was taking his bath. He bleated in his prayers, just before he went to bed. Even Jake had to smile about that.

The adults in the church had a Cantata, which was beautiful. Then the kids did their reenactment of the Christmas story. Afterward, there were refreshments in the basement.

Jake and Marty had never gone overboard on Christmas. They just couldn't afford to buy many gifts. They never bought anything for each other. The children got clothes, one special toy each, and then a game or a toy they could share with each other. This year was no different, except Jake's parents were more extravagant with their giving than in the past. By taking the children to Sunday school and church, they had become more attached to them. Marty's Sunday school class bought her a new study Bible and presented it to her as a gift. Marty wrapped up her Gideon Bible and gave it to Jake for Christmas.

***

Larry Lawrence had begun to purchase his gas and get his car serviced at Jake's gas station. If Jake were not busy, he would have a discussion with Larry about spiritual things. Jake was a little uncomfortable to talk about these things, at least at first. One day, Larry asked Jake if he could come over and talk with him and Marty some evening. Jake was polite, and even though he didn't especially want to do this, he said, "Okay, that would be fine. Just get with Marty to decide what time."

On a Tuesday evening after supper, Larry and Lou came to the apartment. They had left their children with a deacon's family. Larry suggested they all sit at the kitchen table. After about fifteen minutes of small talk, Larry looked at Jake and asked him about his relationship with Jesus Christ. Jake didn't actually understand the question. So Larry asked him if, at any time in the past, he had made a commitment to Christ.

It is true that preachers have their own jargon, which ordinary, unsaved people may have trouble translating. This was the case between Larry and Jake.

Jake said, "Preacher, I am a pretty good man. I don't cheat people. I don't run around on my wife, and I try to take care of my family. I am even nice to my mother-in-law." This brought a chuckle from everyone.

"Do you believe that Jesus is the Christ, the son of God?" Larry asked.

Jake shrugged. "I guess I do, or I wouldn't go to church."

Larry then went through the steps of salvation. Jake affirmed his belief, and that he was a sinner. He even said he repented of his sin. Then Larry asked him if he had ever been baptized for the forgiveness of his sins.

"Well, no, Preacher," he said. "I don't think I need to do all that."

Larry picked up Jake's Gideon Bible and opened it—he had learned in the seminary that it was best to use the prospect's Bible whenever possible. Larry read several passages where Jesus spoke of baptism and then from the book of Acts, where people were converted to Christ. He spoke of a man who was baptized out in the wilderness on the road down to Gaza. He also showed him in Acts where a jailer and his family were baptized by Paul and Silas one night in Philippi. All the while, Marty was following along in her new study Bible.

Larry assured Jake that he didn't want to overload him with too much at one time; he wanted to give Jake the space he needed to think about these things. Larry said, "Let's have prayer before we leave. Then you just think about what we have read in God's word."

Later that night as Marty was on her knees by the bedside, she felt a warm body next to her. It was Jake, on his knees holding her hand as she prayed.

***

Satan had been very active the following week. He tempted Jake with beer and pretty girls. He tempted him with cranky customers who could not be pleased. He tempted him with his own balky car that needed a new battery. But Jake won all these battles.

Prayer is a mighty weapon. That night, as Jake joined Marty in prayer, something began to happen. They were one flesh that evening, just as the Bible says. Jake wanted to please his wife more than anything else from that night on. He was determined to go to church that next Sunday, and this time, he was going to really listen.

(12)

There was one thing that stewed in Jake. And he had a difficult time getting past it; in fact, he simply couldn't. How could God have let his brother die in an auto accident at such a young age? George Edmonds had been such a fine, handsome young man with a great personality. He had planned to become a doctor. It just wasn't fair. Jake knew of at least a dozen people who should have died. The drunk who T-boned George's car should have died, but he didn't. No, for Jake, it was not fair and it was God's fault.

Jake could not let this go. He also could not understand his parents' attitudes. They had gotten over their feelings of anger. They had even forgiven that drunk who took George from their family. Jake vowed that he never would forget or forgive.

On the other hand, some people seemed to be

naturally able to forgive, to be kind and move forward—like his wife, Marty. She had always been a loving person.

Marty had moved past her rotten teen years. She had forgiven her father for abandoning her and her mother. She had forgiven her mother for allowing men to make advances toward her. Now she wanted her husband to become a more loving, kind, and forgiving person. She also wanted her mother to defeat her addiction to alcohol.

Jake's hatred toward the man who had killed his brother was like a cancer. It was killing him slowly. Marty knew that Jesus Christ was the only one who could heal and change Jake.

There were two people whom she wanted to lead closer to Christ. These two people needed to overcome obsessions in their life. Her mother needed to overcome her addiction to booze. Jake needed to overcome his fixation with the man who took his brother away. They were a part of Marty's daily prayers.

She had begun to realize how essential prayer was to her everyday existence. After her daily devotions and prayer, she felt a peace that she could not understand or explain.

Every Saturday evening, she gave her mother a call and invited her to church. Helen always gave a feeble excuse. However, one Saturday evening just before Easter, Helen said she planned to come to church the next day.

***

Sunday morning was as usual with some hustle and bustle around the house as the children were fed and dressed. Jake, Marty, and the children arrived at church just a little earlier than normal. Helen was not there yet. Marty sent Maggie and Jay into their classrooms. Jake was talking with some of the men in the vestibule.

Just as Marty was about to give up waiting and go inside, Helen drove into the parking lot. Marty met her at the front door and noticed the scent of cheap whiskey on her mom's breath. Marty quickly took her aside and told Jake she was going to see Helen to her class, one for the older ladies in the church. Marty asked the teacher if she could just stay with her mother that day, as she was new to the church. It was no problem for the teacher. Marty slipped her mother a piece of chewing gum before they chose their seats around the table.

Fortunately, Helen was not drunk, though she had taken a shot of whiskey before she left the house to bolster her courage. All went well in the class. Helen didn't say anything, and everyone was very friendly.

Larry's message that morning was about people who had lost their way. He said sometimes they found themselves on a way that seemed right to them but was very dangerous. He spoke of a broad, smooth way along which many people were traveling. However, he pointed out that just because many people were on that road did not make it the safest route. As a matter of fact, Jesus said it led to destruction.

Marty thought, *Yes, I was on that road for many years and have only recently found the right road.*

Larry continued to say that the right path had a very narrow entrance, and it was difficult to enter. It was so straight and narrow that few people find it.

At the end of the service that morning, Brother Lawrence asked everyone to take the hand of the person sitting next to them. He then gave these instructions: "Say a silent prayer for the person whose hand you are holding." While the organ played softly, everyone was in silent prayer for each other. A poignant moment.

During this silent time, unbeknownst to Marty, Helen was remembering the day in the apartment when her daughter had taken her hand and prayed for her. This moment also meant so much to Helen, and the tears streamed down her face.

Marty looked at her mom, puzzled. The only time she could ever remember her mother crying was when one of her boyfriends had mistreated her. But these were far different tears. Helen was hurting, but on the inside. She had a longing for something that she could not fathom.

The service that morning had also touched Jake. He'd often thought about what Larry had told him that night when they'd all sat around their kitchen table. This service had him thinking again, long and hard.

(13)

That afternoon, Jake asked Marty if she could help him with scripture in the Bible. She went to the bedroom and retrieved both of their books.

Jake found a slip of paper in the Gideon Bible with all the scripture Larry had given them the evening of his visit. Jake carefully read each one of them and pictured in his mind what it must have been like in each of these scenarios. He thought to himself, *If a commitment to Christ was so essential as to include baptism, then that was what he was going to do.*

Larry's sermons had really begun to hit home. Jake's attitude about the church began to change for the better. However, he still held bitterness against the man who had killed his brother. But it was not as hurtful as it had once been.

He did not confide in Marty about what he planned to do very soon. Marty was pleased that almost every night Jake knelt beside her when she prayed before slipping into bed. He never prayed out loud. But Marty's prayers were so sincere and sweet it gave him a lump in his throat.

Larry came into the station for gas and an oil change that week. He bought himself and Jake a soda and shared some small talk. Suddenly Jake blurted out, "Preacher, I want to do what those people did that you read about at our house that night."

Larry momentarily looked surprised, then a wide smile crossed his face. "Well, Jake, that is fantastic."

"Yes, I have just got to change some things, and I believe Jesus can help me do that," Jake said with a determined voice.

The next Sunday morning, Jake insisted that the family be ready for church a half hour sooner than normal. When they arrived at County Line Church, he told Marty to take the children to class and he would join her in Sunday school.

Jake found Larry in his study. The preacher questioned him and felt confident that Jake knew what he was doing, and he told him so.

At the invitation, Jake could sense Marty's surprise when he boldly stepped forward. Larry took his hand and hugged him.

Jake stated his belief in Jesus Christ and was immersed into Christ.

He remembered the sermon from several months before, where Larry said the blood of Christ wiped the slate clean, and one could start afresh.

But he knew there were still things he'd have to overcome. Money or lack of money was still a problem. He still had acrimony toward Jim Rodgers, the man who killed his brother.

People do not change suddenly.

***

Jim Rodgers lived in town. Jake would see him from time to time. Sometimes he would see him in a grocery store or when he drove past the station. It always brought back some feelings of anger.

Jake had been a little upset with his parents because they only collected from Jim Rodgers' insurance. They never sued, although they could have taken him for every cent he had and would ever have. Jim did not do any jail time. He was still on probation, and he had finally gotten his driver's license back. But Jake thought, *George is still dead.*

(14)

One Sunday, Larry preached from Malachi 3:10 on tithing. Now Jake didn't believe in tithing; he believed more in the idea of "charity begins at home."

In his sermon, Larry made the statement, "You can't outgive God. Because God shovels in and Christians shovel out. And God has a bigger shovel."

Jake thought that was a catchy saying, but it just wasn't good economics.

One Saturday night, Marty and Jake were on their knees beside the bed, ready to pray. Marty said, "Honey, have you ever thought that we ought to tithe your income?"

For an instant, Jake almost got angry. *We're barely keeping our heads above water now!* But he didn't speak his thoughts, and instead took a deep breath and said, "Let's think about it and pray about it."

Jake was maturing in the Lord.

About a week after the discussion about tithing, Henry Jenkins, the owner of the station, came to work and gave Jake his weekly pay. He always paid Jake in cash inside a small manila envelope.

Jake took the envelope home and sat at the kitchen table, counting out the money. He counted seventy-five dollars and fifty cents after deductions. With a pencil and paper, he figured what a tenth of that would be: seven dollars and fifty-five cents. He also calculated the utility bill that was due next week, as well as grocery money and gas money. It was going to squeeze him to tithe. He sat back in the chair and thought about it . . . and was still thinking about it when Marty and the children came in from playing at the park.

Marty saw the money on the table and asked Jake what was going on. He smiled at her and said, "I was just figuring our tithe."

She bent down, put her arms around his neck, and kissed him on the cheek. "Let's do it. Let's try it for six months just like Larry said in his sermon."

As the offering plate came around that next Sunday, Jake put an envelope in the plate with seven dollars and fifty cents in it. That week, Jake cut back on his sodas and his candy bars. For the next four

Sundays, he put that envelope in the offering plate. He had never felt happier in his life about giving up some money. He had also begun to round the tithe up to eight dollars.

The strange thing was that at the end of the month, he had more money in his pocket than he'd ever had since being married. Jake gave the extra money to Marty to put in a safe place. She stashed it in a coffee can in the freezer. In the next three months, the money began to accumulate at a faster rate. Jake eventually went to the bank and opened a savings account.

In just six months, they had saved over a hundred dollars in the bank. And they had not taken any food from the family table to do so. God was keeping his promise found in Malachi 3:10.

<h1 align="center">(15)</h1>

One day at the end of September, Henry Jenkins came to the station and said, "Jake, I need to talk with you. Can I come to the house tonight?"

Jake readily agreed, but spent all afternoon worrying about what Henry had on his mind. Was he about to be fired? He couldn't think of anything he had done wrong. He had worked for Henry for almost eleven years.

Henry arrived after suppertime. Since Marty was still clearing the dishes, Henry and Jake sat in the living room to talk, although the children were enthusiastic about having the attention. Not much talking was done until Marty finally finished with the cleanup and took the children to their room to play.

Henry began, "Jake I have known you and your whole family a long time." He paused and cleared his throat.

Jake tried not to show his worry about what was to come next. But he was definitely thinking, *Oh boy, here it comes. I am about to get the axe.* He waited, holding his breath.

"Jake you're a hard worker and a pretty sharp young man," Henry continued. "My wife and I are not getting any younger. I'm seventy-five years old. The winters up here are about to kill us. We are going to go to Florida for the winter from now on."

Henry wanted Jake to run the station completely, which included taking care of the books, ordering supplies, and depositing the money in the bank. It would be just like he owned the business, Henry said. Jake didn't know what to say. He thought it sounded like it might be more than he could do, even though he had actually done all of this at one time or another, except keep the books. *Well, I'm not getting fired. And I can do that work. This isn't so bad at all.*

Before he could even respond, his boss then offered something even better. Jake couldn't believe his ears when Henry said, "Of course, this will mean more money for you. I will raise your pay to one hundred dollars per week, and any money for labor that you do on anyone's car, you get to keep for yourself."

Jake was almost in shock. Instead of being fired, he was going to have a significant pay raise. He had a lump in his throat and felt a tear forming at the corner of his eye. Fighting the urge to wipe it away, he quickly excused himself and went into the bathroom. There, in that cramped little bathroom, Jake wiped his eyes, blew his nose, and washed his face. When he came back into the kitchen, he told Henry that he believed he could handle the new assignment.

Jake could hardly wait for Henry to leave so he could tell Marty about their good fortune.

That night at bedtime when they were on their knees in prayer, Jake prayed. This was the first time he had attempted to pray aloud. It was a simple, faltering prayer of thanksgiving . . . and for strength to do the job with which he had been entrusted.

The next morning at the breakfast table, Jake asked Marty if she could help him with the books, and offered to pay her a little for her efforts. She, of course, said she would help him. "After all, I am your helpmate, you know." Even though Marty had not finished high school, she was very good with numbers.

A couple of months into his new position as the gas station manager, pump jockey, and mechanic,

Jake knew he had found his niche in life. Marty was doing a fantastic job with the books as well.

The Jake Edmonds family was now thoroughly active in County Line Church of Christ. They had started attending all the services and were learning more and more about their savior. It was a happy time, except that Marty's mother was drinking worse than she ever had. At least her "boyfriends" didn't come around anymore . . . . because she couldn't support their habits and hers too. However, she refused to go to church, even though Marty invited her every week.

<h1 style="text-align:center">(16)</h1>

Two months after taking on his new position, Jake began to search for a house to rent. They had saved enough money to make a move; all they had to do was find the right place.

They put the word out that they were looking for a place to rent. Larry Lawrence even announced it from the pulpit. They searched the paper every day.

During a drive around town after church one Sunday afternoon, they passed an old farmhouse about three miles outside of town. It had a "For Sale by Owner" sign in the yard. They walked around the house and looked in all the windows. It looked to be in better shape than their apartment and had three bedrooms and a nice kitchen. They wrote down the phone number and talked about the house all the way home. They couldn't buy it outright, but perhaps the owner would consider renting it to them.

The next day when he had some slack time at work, Jake called the number. A lady answered and said the house belonged to her mother, who was in a nursing home, but she was handling her mother's affairs. Jake asked her if she would be interested in renting the house because he was sure he couldn't afford to buy it. After a pause, the lady said she didn't think so, but she would talk to her mother. He gave her his number at the gas station and asked her to call him when she knew more.

Two days later, Jake got a call from the lady. She said her mother wanted to talk to Jake before she made a decision. Of course, he was happy to oblige. She suggested that he go to the nursing home on Sunday afternoon and ask to see Mrs. Anna Thomas.

The trip to the nursing home turned out to be a family affair. They all headed there directly after church. Jake went to Mrs. Thomas's room while Marty and the children waited in the lounge.

When he walked in the room, there was a tiny lady with snow-white hair and bright blue eyes sitting in a rocking chair. She wore a pink housedress and a beautiful smile, which immediately put Jake at ease. As he spoke with her, he let it slip that his wife and children were with him. Mrs. Thomas immediately interrupted him—she wanted to meet his wife and kids.

There was an immediate connection between this little lady and the children. They sat on her bed and talked to her as if they had known her all their lives. After about half an hour, Mrs. Thomas looked at Jake and said, "I would be proud to rent you my house. I will take one hundred dollars a month."

When Jake asked her about the deposit, she said, "That won't be necessary. I am a good judge of character. I trust you."

Jake and Marty could hardly believe their ears. It was all falling into place so quickly.

Within six weeks, Jake and his family were moved into the farmhouse. The kitchen had been renovated a couple of years before, and the house had a new gas furnace. Jake's parents and some men from the church helped them move. They had a lot more room and actually could have used some more furniture . . . but that would have to wait. And they were fine with that.

(17)

Larry gave a sermon one Sunday about forgiveness. It struck a nerve with Jake. Larry quoted a scripture where Jesus said that people would be forgiven as they forgave others. Jake knew he was supposed to forgive others; he had heard that enough from his parents. But still, he could not forgive Jim Rodgers, the man who had stolen his brother from him. Then he heard Larry say, "One way of getting over bitterness is to do a good deed for the person whom you can't forgive." Jake thought, *There is no way Larry can understand how I feel.*

In a small town, people talk. Word had gotten back to Larry about how Jake's brother died, and how Jake had held a grudge against Jim Rodgers ever since—ten long years.

On Thursday afternoon of that week, Larry came into the station for some gas. As Jake was filling the tank and checking the oil, Larry pleasantly chatted away, but then abruptly stopped midsentence. Jake's face had suddenly clouded up. He tried hard not to snap at Larry, but his words were clipped: "How can you possibly know anything about forgiving someone who had done something horrible to you?"

Surprised by the subtle anger in Jake's voice, Larry eyed Jake for a moment, then laid his hand on Jake's shoulder. "I have plenty of time; if you have a moment, let's sit down at your desk. Let me tell you a true story."

Into the station they went.

Larry sat in his chair, leaning his elbows on his knees, and looked directly at Jake as he spoke. "I don't talk about this much, but my folks ran a little country store over in Ohio. Everyone in the community loved my folks. They let people buy groceries on credit and were friendly to everyone.

"One day, when I was ten years old, a couple of men came into the store just as my folks were closing up. They pulled out guns and demanded money, which my dad gave to them. Actually, my dad would have given them money even if they hadn't had guns. It was the way my dad was. All those criminals had to do was ask."

Larry paused, which caused Jake to tense up, not sure if he wanted to know what happened next.

With tears welling up in the corners of his eyes, Larry continued. "They shot both of my parents. They killed my mom and dad for a few measly dollars." He paused again to regain his composure. "They robbed my parents of money, but worse than that, they robbed me of the two most loving people I ever knew.

"Now, Jake, with the help of all the people in the community, they tracked down those two murderers. One of them died in prison. The other one is still behind bars. I want to tell you something, my friend," he said as he pointed at Jake. "Until I came to Christ, I hated those men and refused to forgive them. Let me tell you, it just about killed me. It was like a cancer. But my Uncle Bud and Aunt Mary raised me right and helped me to finally forgive these men. When I turned sixteen, my uncle told me if I was old enough to drive like a man, I was old enough to also forgive like a man. So we went to the prison, and I talked to the one who actually pulled the trigger."

He had Jake's full attention.

Larry told how he had taken a Bible to the man for a Christmas present. He said he gave it to the guard to examine, and then was able to hand it to the man. He'd looked the prisoner in the eye and said, "I forgive you for taking my mom and dad from me. I will never forget that horrible day, but I will forgive you because Jesus has forgiven me."

Jake had no words; he'd not anticipated this story at all. He was completely moved.

Larry continued in a gentle tone. "Now Jake, I am asking you to forgive Jim Rodgers. You must forgive him if you are to overcome Satan." He then took Jake's greasy, oil-smeared hand in his, bowed his head, and prayed for Jake as no one had ever prayed for him before. Larry asked God to soften Jake's heart so that he could forgive this man. He spoke of the forgiveness of Jesus as He hung on the cross asking His father to forgive those who had nailed Him there.

As the last amen was said, both men were in tears, refreshed and cleansed by the moment. Jake also felt a new, stronger bond with the preacher—Larry really did know how he felt.

Now, there was something Jake had to do. He had to try to forgive Jim Rodgers for the death of his brother George.

(18)

One evening after supper, Jake was reading his old Gideon Bible—Romans 12:17-20, specifically. His eyes could barely believe what the words were saying to him.

"Do not repay anyone evil for evil. Be careful to do what is right in the eyes of everybody. If it is possible as far as depends on you, live at peace with everyone. Do not take revenge, my friends, but leave room for God's wrath, for it is written. It is mine to avenge; I will repay, says the Lord. On the contrary: If your enemy is hungry, feed him; if he is thirsty, give him something to drink. In doing this, you will heap burning coals on his head."

Jake read that passage again very slowly. It was speaking directly to him about what he must do concerning Jim Rodgers. He had tried to push Jim out of his mind. Jake thought if he didn't think about him at all, then he wouldn't think bad things about him. But it wasn't working.

Jake looked up Jim Rodgers in the phone book. He saw by the address that he lived on the seedy side of town.

After work the next day, Jake drove slowly through that neighborhood and found the house. It was a pretty pitiful-looking house. It needed paint, and a front window was covered with plywood. The screen door was hanging by a single hinge.

Jake didn't stop. But he circled the block a couple of times.

Back at home, Jake examined Romans 12:17-20 again. Like an attorney, he was looking for the loopholes. He found none.

Jake was maturing in the Lord, for that night as he and Marty knelt beside the bed, he asked her to pray for him concerning Jim Rodgers.

He also did some detective work and tried to find more information on the man who killed his brother. The druggist in town told him that Jim Rodgers lived with his widowed mother in that dilapidated house. Jim's mother was a sickly woman and considered an invalid. From all indications, Jim was her only caregiver.

Jake was aware the next move was up to him. He needed to work up some courage.

He confided in Marty, who hugged him for a full

minute before she spoke. With a gleam in her eye, she said, "You know what you have to do, don't you?" It was more of a statement than a question.

The next evening, Jake saw Jim's old Ford parked in the drive by the house. He parked out front and said a short prayer for strength.

Jim answered his knock at the door. It was the first time in ten years they had seen each other up close. Jim had steel-blue eyes with a sharp nose; he was starting to go bald, and needed a shave.

Jake introduced himself, but if the name registered, Jim didn't show it. Jake asked if he could come in. He was led into a small living room with well-worn, but clean furnishings. A tiny lady with stooped shoulders sat in a wheelchair next to a gas heater. A TV sat in a corner of the room, a snowy picture on the screen. Despite the bad reception, Jake could tell that *Gunsmoke* was on. He introduced himself to the lady, who said her name was Geraldine. But Jake called her Mrs. Rodgers out of respect.

Jake told them he noticed that the house was in some disrepair and wondered if there was anything he could do to help. He asked if he could replace the window and put a couple of new hinges on the screen door. He quickly added that he just wanted to help out, and it would cost them nothing. Jim and his mother were a little embarrassed at first, but finally politely accepted his offer. He made an appointment to try to get it done the next week.

Now, in the back of the Jim Rodgers's mind was the thought that they would never see this man again. No one had assisted them in many years. His mother received a small Social Security check. Jim picked up odd jobs but didn't have steady employment.

Before Jake left, he asked them if he could have a word of prayer with them, and they consented. Jake's prayer was short but sincere.

Jake went to church early the next Sunday and spoke with Larry in his study before Sunday school. He told Larry what he had done and said he felt really good about it. But he had a favor to ask: could the church help this family as well? Larry said he would take it up with the elders and deacons.

Jake picked up a couple of hinges for the screen door and put them on. He measured the window for a pane of glass. He came back the next evening and replaced the plywood with the windowpane. The house was looking better already.

Now for the painting of the house. Jake asked, "Jim, if I provide the paint, could you paint the house?"

Jim happily said that he would.

With the plan in motion, Jake then called Larry and asked if the church could buy the paint. He was relieved to hear Larry's response: the elders wanted to help this family in any way they could. And so, the deal was done.

Jake and the church provided the paint, brushes, and ladders. Jim painted that house, which had not been painted in close to forty years. In about three weeks, the house gleamed like a diamond.

(19)

Jim came by the station one day and told Jake he didn't know how he could ever repay him. He was moved by the outpouring of support.

Well, it was time for Jake to tell Jim who he was, and how it was actually Jim who had done Jake the favor—by allowing him to do something good for him and his mother.

When Jim heard the whole story, he started to weep. His shoulders shook uncontrollably. Between sobs, he said, "I am so sorry" over and over again. This man's heart was broken.

Jake could not help himself; he put his arms around Jim and hugged him to his chest, patting his back. He found himself saying, "It's all right. It's all right. I . . . I forgive you."

Suddenly Jake felt a huge burden lifted off of him. And he whispered, "Our God is an awesome God. He keeps his promises."

***

The next Sunday at the invitation, Jake walked to the front of the church and told Larry he wanted to say something. Larry gave him the floor.

"Folks, I committed to Jesus some time back, but I did not surrender my whole self. I held a grudge against a man for many years. But this week, I did what the Apostle Paul wrote about in Romans, and I am now a whole person, completely committed to our Lord."

Jake then told the whole story and encouraged others who might be holding a grudge toward another person to "get it right today, because the sun may never rise on you again."

Jake's parents met him at the back of the building and hugged him. His mother was crying. His dad said, "I am so proud of you." Marty gave Jake a big kiss, too, and hugged him all the way to the car.

(20)

In her devotion and prayer the next day, Marty lifted up praise to God because her husband had overcome two great obstacles. He had become a cheerful giver of his money. And he had overcome his animosity toward Jim Rodgers.

Marty now had to concentrate on her mother. Helen Dennis was a tough one. Marty wanted to be kind and generous to her mother, but she did not want to enable her. The alcohol had a powerful hold on Helen. She drank every day. She was not always drunk, but she always had it in her system.

Marty often prayed for her mother until she cried. She invited her to church every Sunday. However, Helen only came on special occasions and to the children's programs.

Jake had once confessed to Marty that he had a hard time praying for Helen. Drunkenness was a sore spot with him.

So Marty kept on praying.

***

There were times when Jake needed a refresher course in forgiveness. About once a month, he would drive by the Rodgers' house just to look at that new paint job and the repaired window. Sometimes he would stop and speak with Mrs. Rodgers. One day he asked her if she ever got out of the house. She smiled and said, "Only to go to the doctor. When I go, Jim has to carry me to the car since we don't have a wheelchair ramp."

Later, as Jake sat in the car, he thought, *Why didn't I notice they had no ramp?* He began to calculate what it would take to build one. When he got home, he took a pen and paper and figured it all out. Since the house was low to the ground, it would not be difficult.

Jake asked one of the men from the church to deliver the lumber needed to build a ramp. Then he called Jim and told him to expect some lumber and hardware to be delivered the next day.

On Saturday afternoon, Jake, Jim, and two other men from the church started on that ramp. By the next Saturday, it was completed.

Mrs. Geraldine Rodgers rolled herself out the front door and down that ramp all by herself. When she reached the sidewalk, she gave a little wave and a big smile. She was one happy lady. It had been years since she had been able to get out of the house on her own.

Jake knew how she must have felt, for he, too, had been set free.

(21)

Alcohol and smoking do not make a good combination. One night, about eleven o'clock, Jake and Marty were awakened by frantic knocking on the door. He told his wife to stay put and went to answer the door. He was surprised to see a sheriff standing there with a serious expression on his face.

The sheriff explained that there had been a house fire and one person was dead. When he gave the address and asked if Helen Dennis lived there, Jake's heart jumped.

He swallowed the lump in his throat and asked, "What about Helen?"

The sheriff assured him that she was okay and had been rescued by the firemen, but there had been a man inside who did not make it. He added that Helen was so drunk that she could not identify the male who had died. Jake had no idea who it was either.

Helen had been taken to the hospital for observation, the sheriff told him. She was in the rehabilitation wing.

Jake thanked him for the information and somberly went to tell Marty the news.

After Jake called his parents to see if one of them could stay with the children, he and Marty dressed quickly and prepared to drive to the hospital. They were on the road in minutes after Jake's mom arrived.

At the hospital, they were led into a small room that looked more like a jail cell than a hospital room. Helen lay in the narrow bed, shading her eyes from the overhead light. A nurse stood like a sentry at the foot of the bed.

Helen would not be able to talk for a while, the nurse told them. She was incoherent. Jake asked Marty if he wanted her to stay, but she said he should go back to the children. She spent the night at her mother's side, alternating between holding her hand, praying, and offering her water, juice, and coffee.

It was later learned the dead man was one of the men that Helen still allowed to visit and stay sometimes. Marty did not know him.

***

The fire was a blessing in disguise for Helen. It opened her eyes to her alcoholism. She was ready for treatment. She stayed thirty days in the rehabilitation wing. There was much discussion about what to do when she got out. She had no home. There would be an insurance settlement. But she needed a place to stay.

Jake and Marty's farmhouse had an upstairs that was only used for storage. Marty asked Jake if her mother could stay with them for a while. There was considerable discussion, but finally Jake agreed. "But there has to be some rules," he added. They agreed there could be no smoking, no alcohol in any form, and no strange men in the house.

They moved Jay upstairs and prepared his old room for Helen. They'd worried that Jay would be upset by this but he thought it was cool. He'd have the whole upstairs to himself.

Helen did not give up smoking, although all her smoking was done outside. Jake and Marty examined everything that she brought into the house. Helen was in outpatient counseling and went to Alcoholics Anonymous three times a week.

She also attended church with the family every

Sunday — that was an unspoken rule. Helen found it was not as bad as she had imagined. The County Line Church did its best to make Helen feel welcome and comfortable.

Jake may have had more of a problem than anyone with Helen. But with the assistance of Marty and her prayers, he was coping.

(22)

September marked one year since Jake had received his promotion. The transition had gone very smoothly. Finances were in good shape at home and at the station as well.

More and more people were bringing their cars in for minor tune-ups, tires, and batteries. Jake was keeping his promise to God as well. He was giving more to the church than he had ever thought possible. He thanked the Lord every night for the blessings he received. Jake had no idea how things could be any better.

But he was about to find out.

In December, he received a phone call that came as a shock. Mrs. Jenkins told Jake that Henry had suffered a stroke and was in the hospital in Florida. Henry wanted to talk to him face to face. Mrs. Jenkins had sounded so serious that Jake closed the station on Saturday and took a plane to Florida on Sunday morning.

Finally, he arrived at Henry's bedside with Mrs. Jenkins standing close by. He found his boss weak but alert.

They said their greetings, then Henry got down to it. "I won't waste words or time. Jake, you know that the missus and I have no children. You are as close to a child that I've ever had. I don't know how long I have on this earth. Mrs. Jenkins and I are fixed pretty good financially." He paused to catch his breath.

Jake had no idea what was coming next. He nodded, waiting.

Henry continued. "Jake, when I am gone, I am leaving you the filling station. I have already made my will. Mrs. Jenkins wants it no other way either."

Mouth agape, Jake was speechless for a full twenty seconds. Then he reached for Henry's hand and prayed for him. It was a beautiful, unfaltering prayer. When he finished, both Henry and Mrs. Jenkins had tears in their eyes.

Jake said, "Mr. Jenkins, I hope and pray you live to be at least a hundred."

***

God answers in strange ways at times. But He never makes mistakes. That night as Jake was on his flight back to Indiana, Henry Jenkins took his last breath. Jake's parents met him with the news at the airport.

Jake was now a businessman. He owned his own gas station. But he needed extra help. He could not run the business, change tires, and do repair work if he had to always stop and fill gas tanks.

He knew a man who had no full-time job. Jim Rodgers was the man.

He went by Jim's house a couple of evenings later. Jim was just finishing cleaning the supper dishes. He told Jim what he had in mind—he was looking to hire someone to pump gas, wash windshields, check oil, and run the cash register while he worked on cars and managed the business in general.

"And I'm wondering if you'd be interested, Jim."

Jim's eyebrows shot up. This was a good opportunity for him. The obstacle was his mom.

"Sure would like the job, Jake. Would it be possible, if it doesn't cause too much disruption, if I could check on my mother a couple times during the day? I just can't leave her—"

Jake held up his hand. "Not a problem. That can be worked out. After all, I am the boss."

The men grinned and shook hands.

(23)

The next week, Jake and Jim began working together in that station. Jim checked on his mother three times during the workday. If she needed him beyond that, she could call him at the station.

Jake was a good boss, and Jim was a good employee. After the accident, Jim had become a recluse. He was ashamed of himself. It was only after Jake had forgiven him that he began to feel alive again.

Forgiveness works wonders—for the one forgiving and for the one forgiven.

Business picked up with all the friendly and efficient service. Coming on the scene were new gas stations where people pumped their own gas for a savings of a few cents. But no one could give service like Jake and Jim. Their customers were loyal, and they responded in kind.

***

Back in the Jake Edmonds household, things were not so good, however. Helen seemed to forget that Marty was the lady of the home. It was true that anything with more than one head was a monster—a household cannot have two heads.

On top of that, Helen "forgot" occasionally and smoked in the house when Jake, Marty, and the children were gone.

Jake could always tell. He had a sensitive nose. One evening, he came home to find Marty and the children outside swinging in the swing that Jake had made for them. He waved at them and opened the front door. The moment he stepped through the threshold, he could smell it. The smoke was thick.

He exploded at Helen, "You burned one house down, and a man is dead because of it!"

He immediately knew he should have put it another, kinder way. But what he'd said was true, and he could not take it back.

When Marty came in, Helen was crying. Helen looked up at her daughter with teary eyes, expecting her daughter to take up for her.

Marty did not. She said, "Mom, you know the rules. You can smoke if you must, but not in the house." She then embraced Helen and said, "You do understand, don't you?"

Later that night in their room, Marty and Jake talked things over. Jake said, "I am sorry I went off on your mom. I know I need to be nicer to her if we are going to guide her toward better things."

At least it seemed AA and the counseling was working with Helen. She had not touched a drop of alcohol since the night of the fire.

Church seemed to have a zero-sum effect on Helen. She enjoyed the ladies' Sunday school class. She enjoyed the singing, special music, and the fellowship. Preaching? Well, not so much. What was it she'd said? "It's too preachy."

Jake responded with, "Well, duh, it's supposed to be preachy, Mom."

(24)

One day when it was slow at the gas station, Jake asked Jim, "How did you stop drinking?"

Jim was silent as he thought, then he said, "Jake, being responsible for taking another man's life brings one to a crossroad. Either you get worse, or you decide *never again*. I will never again bring heartache to another family. I simply made up my mind that I would never touch another drop of liquor." He added with a grin, "It didn't hurt that we were poor, though."

Jake grinned back, shaking his head.

Then Jim's face became serious again. "After your brother died, all my friends abandoned me. You realize your brother was a very popular teenager."

He told how his mother's debilitating illness actually helped him keep his sanity. "I had so much to do for her when she first got sick . . . it kept my mind occupied."

When Jake got home that evening, he suggested to Marty that perhaps they should give Helen some responsibility. They had pretty much waited on her and didn't really let her do much since she had moved in. He told her what Jim had confessed to him that afternoon.

When the children were all in bed, Marty invited her mom to sit at the kitchen table with her and Jake, and she poured her a cup of strong, hot tea. She took the lead in the conversation, asking her mother if she would like to take on some chores around the house. Helen perked up at this and said she would.

They made a list of things to which they all agreed. A couple of meals a week. Laundry every other week. Washing dishes two evenings a week.

And one night a week, she would watch the children while Jake and Marty had a night out. Jake was not sure about leaving the children in Helen's care. But he finally agreed.

There was an immediate change in Helen's attitude. She had never been an early riser, but she started coming out of her room early each morning with a smile on her face. She even did more than was on the list.

Responsibility can be a great healer.

(25)

Marty remained faithful to her devotions and prayer time every day, which she typically did alone in her room. But one afternoon, she asked Helen if she would like to share in her devotion time. Helen hesitated at first, but finally agreed to give it a try.

Marty had been going through the New Testament during her recent devotion times. When Helen joined her, she was getting ready for I Corinthians 13, the great "love" chapter. She read the entire thirteenth chapter aloud. As she read, Helen seemed mesmerized by what it said about love. Especially *love never fails.*

Also . . . *And now these three remain; faith, hope and love. But the greatest of these is love.*

As she listened to what the Apostle Paul wrote about love, Helen realized she had never experienced real love. She had only experienced what the world called love.

But worldly love is nowhere near God's love.

She had heard the preacher talk about it. But it had never registered with her before today. It was amazing that her own daughter had introduced real love to her. After the prayer, Helen knelt down by Marty's chair and hugged her so tightly she feared she might hurt her. Then she kissed her daughter softly on the forehead. Helen had never before initiated a hug or a kiss.

And ever since that afternoon, this became a part of Helen's routine—devotions and prayer with her daughter.

The worship services at County Line Church of Christ were very simple services. There was no pomp and ceremony. No candles. Larry dressed in a suit and tie—no fancy robe. He insisted on being called Larry or Brother. As a girl, Helen had attended a Catholic Church in Lafayette. She was not used to the simplicity of these services. But she admitted that she liked the way it was, because she could at least understand the preacher. He spoke English instead of Latin.

She began to really listen to Larry when he preached. He often stepped on her toes and made her a little angry. But after she thought about it a bit, she realized he was telling her the truth. It was hard to stay aggravated at someone who was telling you the truth.

Larry spoke of the gentle love of Christ, and he spoke of the wrath of God on those who choose to do evil. He spoke of people who would be in hell, which was a fiery pit. And he almost wept when he spoke of this. It was obvious he did not want anyone to go to hell. She liked that in Larry. He was a loving man who called for people to repent.

Helen told herself that there was no way God could forgive her. It was her cigarette that had started the fire that had killed a man. She just knew she was doomed.

At their devotion time the next afternoon, Helen confessed to Marty that she was going to go to hell because she had killed a man.

Marty grabbed her hand and said, "Oh no, Momma. Jesus died so that all your sins can be forgiven."

Helen had a lot to learn about Jesus.

(26)

Marty made a phone call to Larry that evening and told him what Helen had said. Larry was very troubled when he heard this. He left his study and came right on over to the house. He told Helen he really needed to speak to her in private.

Jake and Marty quickly excused themselves and took the children for a ride to the Dog-N-Suds and then the park.

Larry asked Helen if she had a Bible. She, of course, didn't have one, but she retrieved Jake's old Gideon Bible.

Brother Lawrence, as Helen called him, was very patient with her. He went through some scriptures that he thought were important.

Suddenly Helen blurted out, "I just know I am going to hell unless you absolve me of my sins!"

Larry was caught off guard for a moment, but quickly recovered and extended his hands, palms up. He said, "Helen, look very closely at my hands."

As she stared at his hands, he said, "The only one who can forgive your sins is the one who has the nail prints in His hands. Please notice, I have no nail prints. Helen, Jesus Christ died on a cross for my sins and yours. It is His blood that takes away our sins."

Helen was crying now. Her words were barely understandable, as she stammered, "But Brother Lawrence . . . my drunkenness and carelessness . . . *killed* a man. Not only that, I have committed adultery in my life. I am so wicked that God cannot forgive me." She bowed her head, defeated.

Larry took her hands in his. "Hear this, Helen. Jesus can forgive any and all sins. That was the purpose of Him coming to earth."

He said this in such a tone that Helen just had to believe what he said.

Larry went on to tell her about King David, who not only committed adultery but also arranged for the death of the husband of the woman with whom he had committed adultery. However, because he repented, God forgave him, and he was called "a man after God's own heart." She found that fascinating. After having a prayer with Helen, Larry told her to think about all these things. He would be happy to speak with her again if she desired.

Helen Dennis slept soundly that night and dreamed of going to heaven. She was so refreshed in the morning that she mopped the kitchen and swept all the floors—and it was not even her turn to do these things.

(27)

The next Sunday morning Larry Lawrence had a powerful message about the saving blood of Christ. At the end of the service, when the invitation was given, Helen Dennis walked down the aisle between Jake and Marty.

Helen wanted to accept Jesus Christ as her savior. She wanted Jesus to take away her sins. Jake and Marty rededicated their lives and asked the congregation to lift them up in prayer.

Marty remembered the prayer she had prayed for her mother more than a year before, when Helen had come to the house drunk. She had prayed for the Lord to take away Helen's desire for alcohol.

In the next few weeks, Marty saw that Helen had completely changed. She had a different look about her. Helen confessed that she no longer even *wanted* a drink. "I've not felt this good since I was a young girl," she said.

Marty was not surprised, for she remembered the passage of scripture in the Gospel of John, which spoke of being born again of the water and the spirit.

So much had happened to the Edmonds family in such a short period of time. Less than two years before, Jake was struggling to make ends meet. They were living in a cramped upstairs apartment. He hated a man he really did not know. He was stingy and treated his family pretty shabbily.

God had blessed Jake and Marty in ways that could only be counted as a miracle. God had kept his promise, found in Malachi 3:10. This family's blessings were running over.

***

Something had been on Jake's mind for some time. The County Line Church had grown so much that it was overflowing with people every Sunday.

When Larry came to the station one day, Jake asked if they could talk for a minute. They sat down on a bench in the station and Jake handed him a Dr. Pepper. "Preacher, don't you think we need to enlarge the church building? We're bursting at the seams every Sunday."

Now, Jake was not a deacon, nor did he hold any

church office. But Larry's face lit up at the words. "I have been waiting for someone to mention this," he said. "Jake, I am going to ask you to come to the next board meeting and say to the board what you have just said to me."

On a Monday night a couple of weeks later, Jake addressed the elders and deacons about the need for a larger auditorium, a fellowship hall, and a few classrooms.

The idea was well received. The board members had all been thinking the same thing, but no one had ever started the conversation. They appreciated that Jake was the one who had, and they told him so.

Jake's cheeks reddened at the compliment, and he smiled. "I have found that if you step out in faith, God will catch you," he said.

The church had a large building fund just sitting in the bank, so it wouldn't take much of a loan to swing the deal and get things moving. Also in their favor was the fact that one contractor and at least three carpenters were a part of the congregation. In the weeks to come, as they discussed the building program, the men agreed they could do much of the work and save a huge amount of money.

The new building would be built adjacent to the old one. When the new one was completed, the old building would be used exclusively for classes and storage.

When the community saw the men of the church laboring so hard every weekend, new people began to show up for church. Eleven months later, the problem of overcrowding was alleviated. On that first Sunday in the new building, the pews were almost full. The singing had never sounded better, and Brother Larry Lawrence had never preached a better sermon.

God uses ordinary people to complete His missions. Jake was the ordinary person that got the ball rolling, but many ordinary people had stepped up to the plate.

(28)

Jake and Marty were happy to be a part of such a great congregation. But Jake was unhappy with the fact that he had never been able to make any progress in leading Jim Rodgers to the Lord.

Jim and Jake got along so very well at the station, each of them holding up their ends of the bargain. Jim didn't use crude language, nor did he drink at all. He was as honest as the day was long. He also took excellent care of his disabled mother. In other words, Jim was a really good man. However, he didn't want to hear anything about Jesus.

Since Jake now had a good man to assist him at the gas station, he didn't have to be there during all hours of operation. He sometimes left Jim to manage the station by himself. One Saturday, Jake decided to take his family on a picnic and asked Jim to cover at the station, knowing that he could rest assured that everything would be taken care of.

But that evening, as Jake pulled up to his house, there was a state trooper's car and a sheriff's car in his driveway.

Helen was standing on the porch, wringing her hands and looking extremely distressed. Without a word, Marty corralled the children past her mother and into the house. The sheriff met Jake at the car. There had been some trouble at the station.

Jake listened with disbelief as the sheriff explained the situation. Someone had shot Jim and robbed him. Jim was in serious condition in the hospital. According to witnesses, two men had gone into the station and a third man waited in a car. The witnesses said that two or three shots were fired. The men then ran to the car and were gone.

Jake asked about Jim's mother, if she had been informed, and the sheriff confirmed that someone was on the way to her now. Jake then called Larry and told him what had happened. He asked Larry if he could go to the hospital and wait for him. Jake said he would be along as soon as he had talked to Mrs. Rodgers.

When Jake got to the Rodgers's house, a deputy was already inside. Jake didn't bother to knock, and he found Geraldine Rodgers weeping uncontrollably. He offered her a tissue and told her he would take her to the hospital. Bundling her up in a sweater and a shawl, he pushed her to the car and lifted her into the front passenger seat. He left the deputy in charge of the wheelchair.

At the hospital, Jake lifted the frail little lady into a borrowed hospital wheelchair and rolled her to the ER, where Larry was waiting.

No one could tell them anything about Jim's condition. All the nurse would say was, "They're still working on him." However, Jake was quite concerned about Mrs. Rodgers and asked the nurse to please take her blood pressure.

After about forty-five minutes, a young doctor approached them and introduced himself. He said Jim was stable but needed some immediate surgery.

It was a long night at the hospital. Larry had another urgent call to make, but he brought Marty to the hospital. Jake and Marty took Jim's mother into the chapel, where they prayed for him. Jim's mother cried off and on softly for almost two hours. Jim was about all she had as far as relatives. She had an older brother, but he lived in Texas.

In the early hours of morning, the young doctor finally came out and said, "Jim's out of surgery, and he seems to be responding well. He's strong and in good physical condition, which was a plus for him right now."

But it wasn't until a couple hours later, that Jake and Mrs. Rodgers got to actually see Jim.

Other than the tubes, wires, and other apparatus, he looked pretty good. The bullets had missed vital organs. The gunshots were from a small caliber weapon. He had been shot twice, once in the left side and once in his upper left arm. The bullet in his side had entered and exited, missing his kidney and lung by half an inch. His arm was broken, and he had hit his head on the floor when he fell. After the bullet was removed from his arm, the sheriff had taken it for a ballistics test.

Larry had returned to the hospital by this time. Jake knew this shooting was bringing back some bad memories for his brother in Christ. However, Larry seemed to be handling it well. He had learned to live from crisis to crisis. This was what preachers did.

***

Jim healed quickly. He stayed in the hospital five days. He had a cast on his left arm, but there was no infection in either of his wounds. Jim could not fully take care of his mother until his cast was removed. No lifting for a while either.

Some of the ladies from the County Line Church took it upon themselves to assist. Eight ladies, in fact, made a list and took turns doing everything for Mrs. Rodgers that Jim had done. She seemed to enjoy the extra attention and the girl talk.

Jim was bored, however—until Jake came to the house and took him to the station so he could sit on the "liar's bench" and talk to the regular customers.

The sheriff and the SBI were investigating, but so far, they had no leads. The witnesses were able to describe the car, but none recognized it as familiar. Jim said the men wore women's stockings over their heads for masks. They didn't talk much except the one with the gun, who'd said, "Hurry up, move it." Jim figured the only reason he'd been shot was because he hadn't moved fast enough to suit the gunman.

The criminals had made away with only about seventy-five dollars from the cash drawer, according to Jake's calculations. Thankfully, Jim had just put two hundred dollars in the safe.

Jake could hardly believe that those men would have killed someone for seventy-five dollars.

Larry said, "I can believe it."

After two months, Jim was almost back to normal physically. However, he was nervous about being at the station alone, and Jake made sure to be there with him. Occasionally when strangers drove in, they were viewed with suspicion.

(29)

Six months after the robbery, they were still on alert.

A car pulled slowly into the station one day when Jake was tending the pumps. Squinting in the sunlight, he approached the car and asked the driver what he needed. He replied, "A fill-up and an oil check."

Jim was sitting on the "liar's bench" taking a break with a Pepsi. He heard the man's request. There was something in the tone of the voice that caused him to have a sick feeling in the pit of his stomach. He had heard that voice before, but he did not know the man and he did not recognize the car. The hair on the back of his neck bristled as the man made small talk with Jake.

He tried to not look in their direction but to just listen to the man's voice. He was sure he had heard the voice before. He walked behind the counter where Jake now kept a sawed-off, 12-gauge shotgun. He felt the wood and steel under his fingers. He would be ready this time.

Jake walked in with a twenty-dollar bill and made change.

Jim whispered, "Get the license number of that car, but be careful."

Jake returned to the car, gave the man his change, and said, "Have a nice day, sir." As the man pulled out, he recorded the license number.

Jim was already on the phone to Sheriff Randle. When Jake told him the plate number, Jim shared it with the sheriff.

The sheriff's office ran the plate and found the owner of the car was a lady from Indianapolis. The SBI would do some more investigating.

The next morning, an SBI agent came to the station. They were unable to locate the lady who owned the car. They had called, but she didn't answer. They went to the house, but couldn't raise anyone. A neighbor said the lady was elderly and lived alone. Her car was not in the garage. Red flags went up. The agent asked Jake and Jim more questions.

That afternoon, Sheriff Randle came to the station with "good news and bad news." The car had been located down in southern Indiana. It had a flat tire, and no one was around. The bad news was the owner had not been found. They were afraid that something bad had happened to her.

The sheriff returned the next day with worse news.

The lady had been found about a mile from where the car was abandoned. She was dead, shot four times with a 22-caliber pistol. Sheriff Randle said, "They're comparing the ballistics, but Jim, it looks like you and she were shot with the same weapon. This guy has a lot of nerve to come back to the scene of the original crime. If you see anyone who looks suspicious, be careful and give us a call immediately."

Jake and Jim readily agreed with that plan.

Another week passed before the SBI agent returned to the station to confirm that the bullets came from the same weapon. He looked at Jim and Jake with a stern expression when he said, "That man who pulled the trigger is dangerous and probably unstable. He just might be back again." Meanwhile, law enforcement would cruise by the station more frequently.

***

It was near closing time on a Friday evening, and both Jake and Jim were at the station, wrapping things up for the day. Jake counted the money, made out a deposit slip for the week, slipped it all into a bank bag, and headed for the door.

A car had just pulled up to the pumps. Jake did not recognize it as one of the local customers. A large man got out and started toward the front door. As he walked, he pulled a lady's stocking down over his face. Jim was still standing behind the counter, and Jake was standing at the end of the counter next to the cash register — stock still.

Then . . . a flash of silver in the man's hand. A 22-caliber pistol.

Jim's hand was already on the short-barreled shotgun that they kept behind the counter. He had the hammer pulled back as the man shouted at Jake and told him to get face down on the floor.

Meanwhile, Jim's mind was reeling. *No, I will not end up like that poor lady from Indianapolis, and neither will Jake.*

The robber demanded all the money, not just the cash in the bag.

Jake said, "Okay, take it easy. Jim, let him have it."

And Jim did.

He pulled out that shotgun and rested it on the countertop, pointing straight at the man's large belly. There was terror in the man's eyes. A shot rang out. The man had just fired a bullet straight into a can of oil on a shelf behind Jim—barely missing his head.

The next noise sounded like an explosion as Jim pulled the trigger on that 12-gauge. The large man went flying backward and busted the glass out of the door. His body was sprawled half in and half out of the door.

The coroner said he was dead before he hit the floor.

There was a short investigation by the SBI and the sheriff's office. No charges were filed. That was not to say that Jim didn't feel badly about taking that man's life. He did. But he was sure that the man would have killed both of them had he not pulled the trigger.

(30)

Things quieted down in town after that. Jim got to thinking about his close calls with death. Larry made an effort to stop by the station more often just to talk, and they had grown closer as friends. The ladies at the church proved to be very helpful with his mother, and even when Jim was able to take care of his mother again, the ladies still visited her a couple of times a week.

One Sunday morning, as the men were congregating in the vestibule before the services at County Line, Jim Rodgers walked in. The men cheered when they saw him. Jim smiled at the warm greeting, but felt a little uneasy inside.

He was impressed with the services and with the friendliness of the people. But he still didn't think he needed the Lord; he just needed the company. His mother had been the churchgoer when he was small and before her stroke disabled her. She still read her Bible, and he knew she prayed. But that was not for him.

***

One morning when Jim was at work, he got a call from one of the church ladies. His mother was having some sort of seizure. They had called the ambulance. He was to go to the hospital.

Jim never saw his mother alive again. She was pronounced dead at the hospital before he could get there.

Jake pretty much took charge of the arrangements. Larry held a beautiful service, and the church was as supportive as ever. There was a nice crowd of people at the service. She was laid to rest beside her husband, who had been gone forty-two years. Jim was now all alone in that house. But he would never be lonesome if Jake and the church had any say in the matter.

Jim began to attend church pretty regularly. He loved the fellowship and the music . . . and the preaching was okay too.

Now, Jim had a talent that he had kept under wraps for years. He could play the guitar and sing.

However, he had only played and sung for his mother.

One day, he brought his guitar to the station. To entertain himself, he started singing and playing a Tennessee Ernie Ford song, "Sixteen Tons."

He looked up at the sound of applause. Much to his chagrin, his boss was standing in the doorway.

"Man, that was good," Jake said. "Do you know any hymns?"

Jim shrugged. "I know a few. Just give me the key and start it, and I can play it."

"I don't know keys from corn and I can't carry a tune in a bucket. But you need to sing a special at church."

Jim shrugged again and got back to work.

Sometime later that same day, Larry stopped by. Jake encouraged Jim to play and sing for the preacher. After a little coaxing, he played and sang, "I'll Fly Away."

When the song was done, Larry slapped his thigh and then pointed at Jim. "I want you to do a special next Sunday."

With encouragement from Larry and Jake, Jim finally agreed to play a song at church that coming Sunday: "Amazing Grace."

After the service, an older lady came up to Jim and said, "I have never heard that song sung any better in my life. Thank you, young man."

Well, Jim took a hymnal home with him that day, and every few weeks after that, he would perform for the congregation. The songs affected many people. But perhaps, as he learned the words to some of these wonderful old hymns, they had more of an effect on him.

He learned and sang the old tried-and-true songs of faith. "Leaning on the Everlasting Arms." "Standing on the Promises." "Faith Is the Victory." "The Old Rugged Cross."

One Sunday after he had sung "The Family of God" and the invitation was given, Jim came forward. He whispered to Larry, "May I please say something?"

Larry nodded and gestured for him to address the congregation.

After clearing his throat and taking a deep breath, Jim said, "You folks have been the family I never had. I have no earthly brothers or sisters. My parents are deceased. You have been my family these last few months. I want God for my heavenly Father and Jesus as my Lord."

And so, another victory was won that Sunday morning. Another enemy was overcome by the love of the church and the blood of Christ.

Epilogue

Not everyone overcomes sin. Only those who seek God and are willing to overcome will be saved. Some might think they can get away with sins until the day they die. However, the Bible says there are two appointments that we shall all keep. The writer of Hebrews tells us this: "And as it is appointed unto man once to die, but after this the judgment." Hebrews 9:27

We shall all keep our appointment with death . . . and we shall all keep our appointment with the judgment.

John Donne wrote in a poem, "No man is an island unto himself." It is true, for we cannot pass through this world without touching the lives of others. Our victories and losses have influence upon others. As we overcome our own obstacles and adversities, others are affected and drawn into our circle.

And now the bonus story:

More Precious than a Sunset

Foreword

There is an old church hymn in which one of the verses says: *Beyond the sunset, no clouds will gather, No storms will threaten, no fears annoy. O day of gladness, O day unending. Beyond the sunset eternal joy.*

The psalmist David wrote in Psalm 30:5: *Weeping may endure for a night, but joy comes in the morning.* (NIV)

All people desire happiness, but joy comes from the Lord.

The Woman

It was midsummer 1967 on a small Midwestern farm. The woman was slender with long, dark hair pulled back in a ponytail. Her shoulders were slightly slumped, as if she were carrying a burden. Yet she was attractive, with smooth, dark skin, from hours in the sun. She was dressed in faded, cut-off blue jeans, a short-sleeve shirt tied in a knot at her waist, and scuffed tennis shoes. To the casual observer, the woman appeared as young as seventeen or eighteen.

The woman was standing in the barnyard, shading her green eyes as she gazed intently at the sunset. She pretended to be watching the man steering an ancient, faded red tractor toward the barnyard.

However, it was the sunset that caught her attention. She never wanted to miss a sunset like the one that was about to disappear beyond the squat hill on the back forty of this farm. She had read somewhere that sunsets were like snowflakes. No two were ever exactly alike. So far, she had found this to be true.

The man on the tractor was her husband, but he didn't actually farm for a living. He had never seemed to make a nickel from the farm the whole eight years he had owned it. Farming was his hobby when he was away from the research center, where he had worked since graduating from high school. He was a nice-looking man, lean and tall with a farmer's tan. He spoke with a soft Midwestern drawl.

The woman had only seen him angry when his old farm machinery broke down at a busy time of the year. She recalled that he had never spoken harshly to her or the boys. As a matter of fact, he seldom spoke to her at all, unless it was about the farm or something he needed from the hardware store. There was no small talk at the table or pillow talk at bedtime.

The woman staring at the sunset was Marie Jefferson, a mother of three active, young boys. Thinking of them at that moment, she took a survey to see what they were up to.

The youngest, five-year-old Matt, was moving sand from place to place with his toy truck in a sandbox in the yard. The oldest, Mike, who was nine, and Murray, eight, were climbing up in the hayloft. They pretended to be bailing out of an airplane by jumping down into a pile of straw.

She spent hours at a time just studying these boys. The two oldest interacted so well together. There were only thirteen months apart in age. People often asked if they were twins. They very well could have been, as they anticipated each other's thoughts and moves. Matt on the other hand always liked to play alone and make up his own little games, usually with a toy truck or tractor.

Marie loved all three boys as much as she loved anyone or anything in this world—she wished she could say the same about her husband. She supposed she may have loved him at one time, but she could not be sure.

She only remembered that she had just wanted to get away from her parents' home. Sadly, she could not remember ever being truly satisfied with her life.

In her parents' home, she was babysitter, cook, and housekeeper for a brood of younger siblings while her folks worked. She was raised poor, and she certainly had not bettered herself in this ten-year marriage.

Marie was still a babysitter, cook, and

housekeeper. From her husband's meager salary, she had learned to pinch pennies, pay the bills, and secretly hide some away.

Had it not been for the boys, Marie told herself she would have already run away to some faraway place. She longed to find her knight in shining armor and live happily ever after.

Why had she married? She had become pregnant just before graduation in her senior year of high school. Her parents insisted that she marry as soon as she graduated, and the man had said it was the right thing to do. That seemed to be one of his problems, *at least in her mind*. He always wanted to do the right thing. She thought, *He will never do well because of his rigid morality*. He would never bend the rules. He was not a Christian. But she had to admit, as everyone said, "He's a good man."

He was also a very boring man. There was no excitement. He loved his little farm, into which he poured more and more money. He loved his work in the research center. But she was sure he felt toward her as she felt about him. They were intimate several times a month, but there was no passion. No fire. She was sure, to him, it was simply his obligation as a husband.

And so, she longed for a new life somewhere beyond the sunset over that hill.

Today is the Day

Marie awoke one morning a few days later and said to herself, "Today is the day." She looked at the clock on the nightstand, and its glowing red numbers showed six thirty. Her husband had been gone thirty minutes. She quickly packed a few things in an overnight bag, retrieved three hundred seventeen dollars from the coffee can she kept hidden in the freezer. Her man knew nothing of this money. Marie had squirreled it away over a period of ten years from her grocery money.

The boys had spent the night at her husband's parents, who had planned an outing with the boys today. She had at least ten hours for a head start before anyone would realize she was missing.

Marie set the overnight bag behind the front seat of the old Ford station wagon parked in the driveway and tossed her purse on the passenger seat. She checked the gas gauge and saw that it was three-quarters full.

Backing out of the driveway, she pulled to the overhead gas tank in the barnyard and topped off the tank. When she drove out of the barnyard, she turned west, which was the opposite way from which she would normally travel. The road was a narrow gravel road that ran in front of the house. After about a mile, she turned north on State Road 39. From there she took some hard-surface roads till she hit US Route 52, where she turned the old Ford westward once again. She planned to stay off the interstate, but would try to drive west or northwest as much as possible.

The old Ford had many miles on it, but was in good condition. Her man always changed the oil and kept the engine tuned up. He had said many times that he would not be afraid to drive it coast to coast. Perhaps she would give it a try.

Marie drove as fast as she dared. She didn't stop for lunch. She didn't even stop for supper when it got dark. She just topped off the tank, drank a Pepsi from a machine, and checked the oil in the middle of the afternoon.

Marie longed to see her boys, but she had steeled

herself for this occasion. Children were resilient. They would adjust to her absence, even if she never would.

The Man

It was ten p.m. when Frank Jefferson finally called the sheriff's department and said his wife was missing, along with the old Ford station wagon. The sheriff was not overly concerned, and suggested she was likely just late getting back from shopping. Frank said, "No, she said nothing about going shopping. She's missing." Neither her parents nor his parents had seen or heard from her all day. That was unusual, for she always checked on the boys when they were visiting family.

The nearest neighbors lived a half mile down the road, and they did not recall seeing her either. Marie seemed to have just vanished. The sheriff asked about any arguments they might have had. Frank replied that no, as a matter of fact, the last time they had spoken was early that morning, when he had left for work.

He had said, "I'm leaving, babe," and squeezed her shoulder while she was still in bed, half asleep. He recalled she had grunted back, "Have a good day." Those were the last words spoken between them.

Shedding the Evidence

About the time her husband was calling the sheriff, Marie pulled into a gas station which was closed for the night. Not wanting to arouse suspicion, she parked in front of one of the bays. It would appear to passersby that the car was there to be worked on in the morning.

Marie immediately fell asleep across the front seat and had fitful dreams about her boys. They were crying in her dreams, and she couldn't comfort them. Marie was startled awake by the sound of a truck horn on the highway. There was still some time before sunup. She dabbed at the tears on her face and combed her hair before starting the engine.

Back on the road, Marie found a small café at the edge of a nameless burg. She ordered coffee, one egg, bacon, and toast. She stiffened when a state trooper's cruiser pulled in. The officer glanced at the old Ford as he headed for the entrance to the café. Marie was careful to avoid eye contact and pretended to be looking for something in her purse. She left a small tip, paid the cashier, and went to the restroom. After splashing her face with cold water and combing her hair again, she pushed the door open a fraction and peeped out toward the cash register. The trooper was paying for a cup of coffee to go. She applied some lipstick and waited a little longer.

Marie came out when the trooper was out the door, driving out of the parking lot in his cruiser. Then she, too, ordered a cup of coffee and, as an afterthought, a donut to go.

Marie had no idea how long it would be before she would actually become a missing person, and the law would start looking for her. But she knew she needed to have another means of transportation. They probably would be looking for the Ford.

Marie looked in the rearview mirror at the strange woman looking back at her. Was she really running away or was this a dream? No, it was real. But the face in the mirror looked to be several years older than the girl who had left the farm only yesterday.

What would she do when her money ran out? She had never worked away from the house. She had few skills. However, she had learned to type in high school. And she thought she could learn a new skill quickly, but first she needed to get farther away from the farm.

Marie passed a used car lot just outside of St. Louis. The sign said, "We Buy, Sell, and Trade Cars." She turned around and drove onto the lot. A rather fat man who appeared to be in his sixties was sitting in an old rocking chair in front of a shanty of a building. He looked like a "typical" used car salesman, she noted. He was dressed in a green sweater and brown corduroy trousers with a John Deere cap pushed slightly back on his head. He slowly pulled himself out of the chair and walked with a slight limp as he came to the car window, which she had cranked down. He touched the bill of his cap and said, "Howdy, little lady. What can I do for you this fine day?"

Marie said, "I want to sell this fine car."

He looked at her, then he looked at the car. "Okay, what's wrong with it?"

"Nothing is wrong with it, except it has a lot of miles on it. It's old."

"Do you want to trade it in?" He jingled some change in his pocket and rocked back on his heels slightly.

She shook her head. "No, I want cash for it."

"Is it hot?"

She almost cursed but instead just said, "No, I need some cash. And I have the title right here in the glove box."

The fat guy limped slowly around the car, kicked the tires, opened the hood, and stared at the engine for a while, as if he had never seen an engine. He opened the rear door and looked inside. Of course, it was a mess. She should have cleaned out the candy wrappers, potato chip bags, and an old squeeze toy before offering it for sale.

He said, "Let me see your title."

She handed it to him, and the gimpy, fat guy looked it over carefully, glancing again at the car, and said, "I'll give you three hundred fifty big ones for it."

Marie looked a little shocked, like he had slapped her in the face. He was not dealing with an amateur. She had saved up a bunch of money by being sharp. She shot back, "Five fifty."

"Four."

"Four fifty."

He thought a few seconds, pushed back his cap, scratched his forehead, and then said, "Done," as he offered his hand through the open window.

The business was quickly concluded, and she left his little shanty office with four hundred fifty dollars plus the three hundred sixty-four dollars she had in her purse.

Not a Clue

By the morning after his wife left, Frank Jefferson was frantic. What would he do with the boys? They were fussy and kept asking about their mother. He had a cow to milk, hogs to feed, corn that needed to be cultivated one last time. His work at the research center couldn't wait either. There were important tests to conduct. He was never an organized man, and now he was even less organized. Too many things on his mind.

Marie Jefferson's parents were not happy with this situation. They seemed to blame Frank for this turn of events. But he was just as much in the dark as they were. He had never struck the woman. As a matter of fact, he could not remember any kind of serious argument they'd ever had. Frank had sensed some resentment about something, especially in the last few months. But he had never asked her if there was a problem. The dilemma was it could be another twenty-four hours before Marie Jefferson could be officially considered missing and a "missing persons" bulletin put out on her.

Frank tried to think back for a clue as to where she might be. She didn't have any old boyfriends. As a matter of fact, neither of them had any close friends—male or female. He was the only man she had ever dated that he knew of.

Then it began to dawn on him. He did not know the woman who was the mother of his children. He sadly realized he knew more about his coworkers and the men who sat on the "liar's bench" at the grain elevator where he sold his corn than he knew about his own wife.

Riding and Thinking

Marie walked to a nearby service station and asked the young man with a greasy rag in his hand and a smudge on his forehead where the nearest bus station was. He told her there was a Greyhound station a couple of miles down the road, but if she could wait a few minutes, he would give her a ride. He said he had to go pick up a set of spark plugs for a car he was working on.

She was tired, thirsty, and had nothing else to do at the time. She bought a Pepsi from a machine, sat down on a bench, and waited with her purse in her lap and her overnight case at her side.

The trip to the bus station in the old pickup truck was uneventful. The young man was not all that inquisitive, and that was a good thing. Marie gave generic answers to the few questions he asked her. She thanked him as he pulled up to the bus station.

He wished her good luck and drove off. Inside the bus station, Marie realized she did not have a destination in mind, except to go west . . . *to go toward the sunset and beyond.*

Picking up a schedule, Marie studied it for a few minutes. Upon checking prices and destinations, she decided on Kansas City. It was only fifteen dollars and fifty cents to ride from the east side of the state to the west side. It would be a long enough trip for her to get some rest. However, she had four hours to kill before the last bus of the day left. She sat down on a bench and realized she was far more fatigued than she'd thought. She dozed off for almost two hours. She then walked across the street to a 7-Eleven store, where she freshened up in the restroom, which was much cleaner than the one at the bus station. She purchased some Nabs, chewing gum, and a stale peanut butter sandwich for the trip.

Finally on the bus, Marie was relieved that there were only three other people riding to Kansas City. She did not have to have an uncomfortable conversation with anyone. She actually had time to think.

Her mind had never fully left the boys. Marie also wondered how her man was doing all by himself. Was he worried? Was he angry? Was he relieved that she had disappeared? Just what would his attitude be when he understood that she was gone for good? She had no idea.

Running these things through her mind, Marie suddenly became aware of a sobering thought. She knew nothing of importance about Frank Jefferson. He was the man for whom she had cooked, kept house, and slept with for ten years. She had even given him children, but she did not know him. It made her feel kind of cheap. Like a kept woman. But now she was free.

However, like a freed slave, how would she live? She would need to think about this as she rode this big Greyhound westward. It came to her some time later as she was jarred from a restless slumber by a pothole in the road. She would pick up a job or two along the way. She would work her way westward . . . *toward the sunset.*

What Now?

The bus station at Kansas City was not far from the center of the city. In the station was a bulletin board with all kinds of ads on it. She searched it for jobs. She bought a paper called the Kansas City Star. After scanning the headlines and the out-of-state stories, she turned to the want ads and searched for a job. She circled several for dishwashers, receptionist, babysitter, and even a house sitter. But she had no references; she had little experience, and she had no really acceptable clothes to wear for an interview.

Marie found a seedy-looking little motel not far from the bus station. The long-haired, weasel-faced man at the desk said the room would be eight dollars per night if she stayed more than three days. She registered, but used an alias and a fake address. She paid three days in advance to get the cheaper rate. In the lobby, there was a coffee pot, drink and candy machines, and a noisy ice machine. There were three other men and one woman lounging around. They did not strike her as being guests. She learned later that the woman was a housekeeper. But it appeared little housekeeping was ever done. The men were always hanging around but did not seem to have jobs.

The next morning, Marie had a quick shower and drank a cup of very strong coffee from the lobby. She next went exploring and found a consignment shop about a block away.

She was proud of herself as she bought some nice clothes for a good price. Back in her motel room, she changed into an appropriate pale blue dress, which accented her body nicely without being vulgar. She had also bought shoes and a small purse to match. She was ready to look for a job. She selected the most desirable jobs for which to interview that morning. Her first choice was for a job as a receptionist at a Buick-Cadillac dealership.

***

Marie was led into an office with a shaded window overlooking the showroom. The smartly dressed manager with slick, black hair and a thin "cookie duster" mustache pulled the shades. Before starting the interview, he offered her a Coca-Cola, which she declined. How old was she? Marital status? How long had she lived here? Did she have transportation? He seemed interested when she said she had just arrived and was living in a motel.

He sat on the front edge of the desk and leaned toward her more and more with each question. Eventually, to emphasize a question, he placed his hand on her knee, squeezed, and moved his hand up her leg. Marie was from the country, but she saw where this was going. She quickly got up and broke off the interview. This was not her Prince Charming or her knight in shining armor. This man was on the prowl.

Marie had two more interviews that day. None proved to be successful. On her way back to the motel, she passed a café with a sign in the window: "Waitress, cook, dishwasher wanted." It didn't look like much of a restaurant, but she went in anyway and asked to see the manager.

An older lady approached her. *She looks about the same age as my mother*, Marie surmised. Turned out, the lady was both the manager and the owner of the establishment. She seated Marie at a rear booth and pushed a cup of coffee in front of her.

Marie learned that the owner's name was Laura Sloan. She was relieved that Laura didn't ask a lot of personal questions. But she did want to know if Marie had ever done any kind of similar work. Marie lied a little. Yes, she had cooked and waited tables and washed dishes. Well, that was not a lie. She just had not been paid wages to do those things. What she lied about was where she had done it. She just said, "Here and there." Laura let it slide and asked her how soon she could start. Marie was anxious to get started and replied, "Would tomorrow be soon enough?"

Turn the Page

A new chapter began in the life of the woman who had escaped from a farm in the Midwest. The next morning, Marie awoke early and took a bus to the café. She arrived a few minutes before Laura drove up and unlocked the door. The early-morning crowd consisted mainly of men on their way to work. There were factory workers, bus and taxi drivers between shifts, a couple of well-dressed men with briefcases, and a city police officer. But most of the customers were laborers. It seemed most of them knew each other, by first name anyway. It was a regular stop for them, and a place to socialize before the workday began.

One older gentleman named Hank was retired and spent most of the morning leaning on the counter and drinking coffee as he talked with Laura. Marie's job this morning would be cooking. She made eggs over easy, scrambled and well-done, and an omelet now and then. There were also hash browns, pancakes, bacon, ham, and sausage. All that was easy enough for her. The older woman seemed happy with her new cook.

At about ten thirty, the place was pretty much cleared out. Now Laura took over the cooking. She had a set menu for each day of the week. The lunch crowd would know what they were going to have when they came in. The two women worked well together, Laura cooking and Marie waiting tables. She learned quickly that the people liked their coffee cups and tea glasses kept full. The men who came in seemed to like seeing a new face . . . especially a pretty, young face. They left very good tips, for which Marie was grateful.

Late that afternoon, a rather dowdy, middle-aged lady named Joan came in and, without saying a word, put on an apron. She and her husband Fred worked the evening shift. Fred was stoop-shouldered and looked to be several years older than Joan. He washed dishes, swept, mopped, and in general, took care of the maintenance. Joan operated the grill and waited on customers because the traffic was light in the evening.

Laura offered to give Marie a ride to her hotel

room. Marie gladly accepted, as she was worn out. Before they left, Laura called her to the back booth where she dumped all the tip money on the table and began to divide it into two piles. She scraped one pile into an envelope and handed it to Marie, who was starting at her. She could hardly believe it when she heard Laura say, "This is your part of the tips today. You did a real good job." Marie was overcome with emotion. A tear ran down her cheek and fell on her blouse. No one had ever complimented her for anything, at least not that she could remember. And most certainly no one had ever given her money for what she did.

When Laura Sloan let Marie out at the motel, she had a scowl on her face. It was obvious she didn't approve of Marie's living arrangements.

In her hotel room, Marie counted out twelve dollars and fifteen cents from the envelope. Here she was—twenty-eight years of age—and this was the most money she had ever actually earned. She thought, *I didn't even ask how much I was going to be paid per hour.* But she didn't care. She had earned enough to more than pay for the motel room. Plus, she got to eat one meal free.

Marie fell across the bed, content, and was immediately asleep. She was awakened by a siren on the highway. It was twelve fifteen a.m. Undressing, she turned the shower on as hot as she could stand, and showered for a good ten minutes until the water started to run cold. Quickly drying off, she fell into bed, closed her eyes, and silently thanked God for a good day. She also remembered her boys back on the farm. "God, please keep them safe, and comfort them."

Marie got her wake-up call at five a.m. and was at the restaurant forty-five minutes later. By six thirty, the rush was on. Same crowd as yesterday. She began to know by memory what each person would order. It was a pretty happy bunch. Even Marie was happy until she momentarily thought about her boys. She knew they would be well cared for by Frank and both sets of grandparents. However, she was concerned that they would cry for her.

No Word

It was six a.m. when Frank got the boys up and partially dressed. He called his mom and told her he was dropping them off in about half an hour. He asked if she could feed them because he didn't have enough time this morning. He would need to remember to start earlier so he could dress, feed, and drop them at her house in the morning. Since it was summer, he didn't have to get the two older ones ready for school. Frank's mind was going in several directions as he thought about the boys, his work, the farm, and finally, of course, Marie. It seemed she was still last on his mind.

A call to the sheriff's office brought a negative response. No one in twenty counties had seen Marie or that old Ford. Since it didn't appear that a crime was involved, no one was all that interested. The verdict was just a runaway housewife who had grown tired of life on the farm.

***

Saturday and Sunday were light days at the restaurant, so Laura gave Marie every other weekend off. They would take turns on Saturday and Sunday. On her off weekend, Marie rested most of the days. But before sundown, she would walk to a park that had a small creek running through it. There she would sit on a bench, watch the sun go down, and keep vigil until it was dusk.

She had not forgotten about going west toward the sunset, but it was only faintly on her mind these days. However, the boys were never far from her thoughts. She did not miss Frank or that wretched farm. She did not even miss her folks. They had never been close. She had always felt like hired help in both of those houses.

Now, her relationship with Laura Sloan was different. Laura had taken an interest in Marie as no one ever had before. Laura had nagged Marie like a mother over that rundown motel room. They would look for a better place, if she could find one close by.

The Preacher

One Sunday morning, Marie got up fairly early and went for a walk in the same park where she always watched the sunset. She sat on a bench overlooking the little creek. She just sat for a while and silently prayed to God about her situation.

Finally, when she left the park, she turned and went the opposite direction. After walking a couple of blocks, she heard a piano playing and voices singing an old hymn that she had heard long ago as a child.

She remembered the words and sang them quietly to herself as she followed the sounds around the corner to a small, white, frame church building. She paused at the door, and one particular voice caught her attention. It was a beautiful baritone—rich, pure, and strong.

Marie cautiously opened the door and timidly

sat down on a back pew. The man she'd heard was standing down front and was leading about two dozen people in this familiar song: *"I come to the garden alone, while the dew is still on the roses. And the voice I hear falling on my ear, the son of God discloses . . . And He walks with me and He talks with me. And He tells me I am his own . . . And the joy we share as we tarry there, none other has ever known."*

She knew that song. She had heard it sung at funerals, but she had never heard it sung so beautifully before. As she sat there, she became mesmerized by this man in his dark blue suit and tie. He looked to be about thirty-five years old and was ruggedly handsome with thick, black, curly hair, dark brown eyes, and a deeply suntanned complexion. As the song ended, he gave Marie a nod that seemed to welcome her. She returned the greeting with a shy smile and a nod.

It was the first time she had been in a church building in many years. Her folks had never been faithful. She and Frank never had time for the church. But this little church was so inviting, and she found herself enjoying the activities.

It was a simple service. No pomp and ceremony. Marie at first though this man must be the song leader, but after a brief prayer, he walked to the pulpit, opened a Bible, and read some scripture. He then began to speak to the people in a calm, conversational tone. He was not the stereotypical preacher shown in movies or on TV. Every eye was glued to him. Yet Marie thought he was speaking only to her.

He spoke of a people who were wandering in the wilderness looking to go into a promised land. Then he spoke of Jesus, God's only son. He spoke of mercy and grace and forgiveness of sins. Too soon, the service was over.

After a short prayer, he offered an invitation, and they all sang "Just as I am." In the back of her mind, Marie thought, *No, God surely would not want me just as I am.*

Marie shook hands with this handsome man at the door, and they exchanged names. His name was Brock Weston. He gave her a card with his name and the name of the church on it, while inviting her back next week. He seemed genuinely disappointed when she told him she had to work next Sunday. He asked her where she worked. He was familiar with the café, but said he had only been there a time or two.

Marie went back to the park that evening, and she noted the sunset was particularly beautiful to her. It was the end of a perfect day.

***

On Monday morning about ten o'clock, Marie glanced up as another customer came in the door dressed in dark green work clothes and work boots. It was Brock West, the preacher. He sat down in a booth and gave her the same nod he had at church the day before. Since it was about time for the shift to change, Laura asked Marie to wait on this new customer.

He ordered coffee and asked if it was too late for him to have some breakfast. Marie told him that they served breakfast all day long. There were only two other customers in the restaurant, and they were just drinking coffee.

As Brock drank his coffee, he asked Marie if she could sit with him while he ate. Marie didn't know what Laura's policy was on this, so she quietly asked her if she could sit with him, since he had invited her. Laura nodded and said that would be fine. "Take a break."

Brock told her how he had been so happy to see her in the services yesterday. He asked her where she lived and frowned when she told him. He was familiar with that motel. It did not have a good reputation. Marie assured him she was trying to find another place to live, but it would need to be reasonably priced. Brock asked her if she minded if he tried to find her a place. She eagerly accepted his help.

He didn't ask her about her past, which she found refreshing. But for some reason, she also found she wanted to tell this man everything about herself. Maybe she would . . . someday.

Just Coping

Frank Jefferson was coping, with the help of his parents. Marie's parents, William and Jan Holly, were concerned that something really bad had happened to their daughter. They did some sleuthing on their own but turned up very little. She had taken few clothes with her and had left the checkbook. As far as they could see, she had left the house exactly as it was. Just her purse, an overnight bag with three sets of jeans, blouses, and toilet articles were missing. But then, Marie had never been a clotheshorse. Just about all her things were casual, everyday articles.

Both sets of grandparents heaped much attention on the boys. They finally stopped asking about their mother. They got to go places now that they had never gone before. They went to the zoo, a carnival, and to the State Fair. When school started, Mike and Murray settled in and adjusted quite well. Frank's parents kept Matt during the day, and the two older boys when they came home from school.

***

As for Marie, she thought about the boys every single day. She wished she had more pictures of them than the small snapshots in her billfold. She could not risk a phone call to see how they were doing. A call could be traced. She did not want to talk to any of the adults right then. Maybe some time, but not right now.

Marie had younger brothers and sisters, but they had never been close. Marie had just been an older babysitter to them before she left home and married. She figured everyone would soon forget her—like when a person dies, she would eventually be put out of mind.

The Little Flock

Brock Weston came into the café two or three days a week around ten in the morning. Sometimes he only drank coffee instead of ordering a full meal. He would read the paper and ask Marie to sit with him for a few minutes. She found talking to him was so easy. He was a good listener. He came up with bits of humor and wisdom for her to smile over.

Marie never missed a worship service on the Sundays she was off. The services were held at Smyrna Community Church, which was named after the church found in the Book of Revelation. It touted itself as a nondenominational church trying to follow the New Testament pattern found in the Book of Acts. It was established by Brock and six families five years before to meet the needs of disenfranchised people.

Marie later found out that most of these

Christians were considered outcasts by other more affluent congregations. They were recovering alcoholics, former drug abusers, couples in mixed marriages, and divorcees. Marie thought to herself that, because of her circumstances, she would fit right in.

She also observed that they were among the most loving people she had ever met. Every Sunday that she could attend, she was greeted with hugs all around, and kisses from the ladies. No glum, sour people here. They were always smiling, laughing, and pleasant.

Marie found she was learning so much from Brock Weston's sermons. At first, she came mostly because Brock was easy to look at and listen to. But she soon realized she was also coming because her spirit was being fed. This was what had been missing from her life for so many years. She began to thank God every day that He had led her to this place. However, she reminded herself that one day she would move on toward the setting of the sun . . . *someday*.

A New Home

One day, Brock came in and asked her if she would like to look at a place to live when she got off work. She happily agreed, as there seemed to be more and more shady characters hanging around the motel, and she had begun to feel uneasy. The police had even come one night and arrested a couple who were selling drugs from their room.

That evening when she got off work, Brock was waiting for her in his well-used 1956 Ford. The paint was faded and the seats were worn, but the tires were good and it ran smooth as silk. Brock said he was kind of a shade tree mechanic and did his own work on it.

They actually would not have had to drive to the place he showed her—it was only a few blocks from the café. But she enjoyed the ride and the conversation. He stopped in front of a well-maintained blue and gray single-wide mobile home. It was right beside a neat, white bungalow with blue trim in a quiet neighborhood.

Brock opened the car door and escorted her by the elbow to the front door of the mobile home. He produced a key, opened the door, and turned on the light. It was fully furnished and just as neat and clean inside as it was outside.

Marie went through the trailer and looked it over. "It's really nice, Brock, but I doubt if I can afford it right now." She looked down at her feet and sighed.

"How do you know? I haven't told you how much it is," he said, smiling. "Marie, I own this mobile home."

She looked at him with wide eyes, speechless.

"It's true. I was renting it to a man who has taken a job in the next county and has moved. I had it all cleaned up for you. I am asking a hundred dollars per month. I know that is less than what the motel charges you. The only extra expense will be your utilities. As for me, I just want someone nice living here, because, you see, I live in the house next door."

Marie didn't know what to say. Tears welled up and overflowed down her cheeks. She felt the same way she'd felt that first day at work, when Laura had shared the tip money with her. She thanked God under her breath and said, "I'll take it."

When Marie got back to her room, she began to have second thoughts. What was this man's motive? She thought she could trust him, but she was not sure. Besides that, she was beginning to have some deeper feelings toward Brock. What if he had a steady girlfriend and she became jealous of an attractive lady living so close?

Confession

When Brock came in for his coffee the next morning at ten, she sat down across from him, looked him in the eyes, and said, "Are you sure you want to rent me the trailer? Are you sure it's wise?" Before he could respond, she then blurted out, "Let me confess some things to you."

Brock had a puzzled look on his face, so she continued, "I ran away from my husband and children back in Indiana." It sounded strange to her, coming from her own lips. It sounded almost evil. She had not even told Laura this. "I need to confess that I have deeper feelings for you than I have ever had for anyone in my life. Brock, I think . . . I think . . . I love you."

There it was, all out in the open.

Brock looked like it didn't register with him for a moment. Then after a long pause, he said, "I'm sorry you felt you had to run away from your family, Marie. I have no idea why you would do such a thing, but you must have had a good reason. Let me also confess . . . I am glad you ran to this place. I hope I can rescue you from whatever it is you are fleeing."

He went on, "God has called me to rescue people, to snatch them from Satan and bring them to Christ." He did not mention anything about what she'd said about thinking she loved him. They both quickly finished their coffees without looking at each other, and without another word.

Slowly Changing

The oldest Jefferson boy, Mike, had his mother's disappearance all figured out in his mind. He just knew she had left because of him. He had misbehaved one day, and when scolded, he told her, "I hate you and I wish you were dead." He didn't realize that all children say or at least think this at some time or another. It ate at his heart.

One day around sundown, for the first time in his life, Frank Jefferson sat down and actually talked with his children. Mike had always been a little rebellious. Murray was somewhat of a follower and looked up to his older brother. Little Matt, the loner, still nearly always played by himself.

Mike was sure he had put a spell on his mother. Lately, he had become rather depressed. Frank sat and not only spoke to the boys—he listened to them over ice cream and cookies. Frank realized he did not know his boys any better than he knew their mother. But he vowed to remedy that. When this session ended, all four of the Jefferson men were in much better spirits. Good things could come out of bad things that happen. People could change. Frank was slowly learning . . . and changing.

Transition

The church where Brock preached could not afford to pay him a large salary. So two days a week, he filled in at the oil field as a roughneck, a person who does the heavy work at the oil rigs. He liked this work; it kept him physically fit, and it was outside. He was also able to witness to the other men at the drilling site. Brock made enough on the side to live comfortably, and he was wise with his money.

Marie missed Brock when he didn't come to the café due to his other obligations. On those days, everything just seemed to be out of sorts for her. But she was happy with her living arrangements.

Moving into her new home was easy. She only had some clothes to move. Laura helped her set up housekeeping with a few dishes, pots, pans, and cleaning supplies.

Brock was a perfect landlord. He never bothered her. He didn't want the church folks to think there was any hanky-panky going on. He only saw her in church or at the café.

Actually, it began to bother Marie some. Because she really did have deeper feelings for this man. She wondered if the other single ladies in the church felt like she did about him. She had no right to have any kind of emotional feeling toward him. After all, she was still married with children.

Then one day at the café, Marie asked Brock if she could talk with him in private. They made an appointment for that evening at her trailer. She prepared a nice late supper for them—spaghetti with meat sauce, salad, and iced tea. After supper, they both did the dishes, and then she was ready to talk. They sat at the table, and she told him all about her previous life. She told him about her folks, her marriage, her children, and her life of living with a man she didn't love.

Brock sat and listened. He did not interrupt nor did he sit in judgment. He just looked into her eyes and listened as no one had ever listened to her before. She only paused long enough from time to time to cry and wipe tears from her eyes with the handkerchief he produced from his pocket. She thought this man must have been a Boy Scout, because he always seemed to be prepared.

Strangely enough, Brock offered no solution to her confession. He only said that she should remember that he and the Lord would always be there for her.

Before he left that evening, he had a prayer with her and gave her a brotherly hug. And then he was gone. She found herself wishing he had taken her in his arms and kissed her. She knew that would have been wrong, but still she wished for it.

She could not explain it, but she felt a release by telling Brock all about herself. She knew he would not blab it to anyone. One day, she would get around to telling Laura what she had told Brock.

Marie did not like living in limbo as she was doing. She needed to move on with her life. Hiding out was not good. She was always looking over her shoulder, wondering when she would be discovered by someone from back in Indiana.

A few weeks later, Marie asked Laura if she could talk with her in private. That evening, Laura went to the house with Marie after work. There, over a glass of iced tea, Marie told Laura the story of her life, just as she had told it to Brock.

Laura asked a few questions and then confessed

that she, too, had been in a very bad marriage. Her husband had been an alcoholic who mistreated her and used her. Fortunately, they had no children to be hurt by this bad marriage. Laura went on to say he was killed in an automobile accident about five years before while driving drunk.

It seemed this little talk by the two woman had cleared the air, and they both were relieved. There were no secrets between them now.

***

Marie saved enough money to call a divorce lawyer. But before she did, she talked with Brock, asking for his opinion. He agreed that it would be wise to settle the matter once and for all. He also offered to go with her, if she wanted him to. It had been almost a year since she had left Frank and the boys. The next day, she looked in the phone book and found an attorney who specialized in family law.

During her discussion with the attorney, he told her, "You realize that you will never get your boys back unless their father dies."

What was it he'd called it?

Abandonment.

He made it sound so evil and heartless that she began to cry. Right on cue, Brock produced a clean handkerchief. The attorney explained that was what the law called it: abandonment.

In the car, Brock prayed with her while holding her hand. It meant so much to her that he was with her in this time of need.

Marie thought about her predicament all that sleepless night. The next day, she called the attorney and asked him if she could start the proceedings. It would cost her one hundred fifty dollars to get started and another one hundred fifty when he had all the papers ready. He said he would start as soon as he had the retainer in hand. Two days later, the process began. This took much of the money she had saved, but it didn't take much for her to live on. She had always been a wise manager of money.

After All This Time

Frank Jefferson was surprised when he opened the kitchen door, and there stood Jerry Foster, a deputy sheriff he had known since high school. Jerry had a piece of paper in his hand and a professional look on his face. He gave Frank the paper and said "Sorry I have to serve you this." It was an official court summons for divorce. The document had Frank's name and the name of Marie Holly Jefferson on it. So at least he knew she was alive. The document said he must appear in court if he wished to contest the divorce.

Deputy Foster got back in his car and left. Frank sat down at the kitchen table and read the document again, slowly. As it registered with him, he put his head in his hands and for the first time since Marie left, he wept. Why, he did not know. It was not that he loved Marie that much. It was more that he felt he had failed as a husband. Marriages were not supposed to fall apart; they were supposed to last until death took one of the partners. He had failed miserably.

The next day, he sat in the office of Robert Patterson, Attorney at Law. He was an old friend of the family, and he trusted "Bob," as he called him. "What about the boys?" Frank asked him. Bob said there would be no way Marie could get the boys. She had abandoned them and left them with him. That news came as a relief to Frank because the four of them had bonded in the last few months. He had spent more time with them this last year than he had spent with them in the previous five years. He was learning to be a father—a good father. He learned more about this difficult task every day. But he *was* learning, and he was getting better at it.

Something New

Something new had also developed with Frank. One night, about two months after Marie left, a preacher and his wife came to visit. He was a pleasant, middle-aged man with a warm smile. His wife was an attractive, quiet lady. Frank learned that their names were Jackson and Janet Saunders. They told him to just call them Jack and Jan.

While Jack talked with Frank, Jan took the boys aside and played a game of Hide the Thimble with a tube of lipstick from her pocketbook. Pretty soon, they were laughing and having a big old time.

Before the Saunders left, Jack called Jan and the boys back in the kitchen where they joined hands, and Jack prayed for the Jefferson family. After they left, Frank said to the boys, "That was really nice, wasn't it?" The boys nodded in agreement. The next Sunday, the Jefferson men were in the large Christian church where Jack preached. Frank thought it was a very nice service, and the boys were overjoyed because they had a children's church service.

Frank had stopped working on Sundays not long after Marie left. He needed this time with his little guys. Then every Sunday after Jack and Jan had come calling, they were off to the Cedar Grove Christian Church on State Road 39.

There was an attractive lady who played the piano at Cedar Grove. Frank thought he knew this lady; she looked so familiar to him. The bulletin gave her name as Joy Silvers. She reminded him of a girl he had gone to grade school with many years ago. One Sunday, about three months later, he asked her where she had attended grade school. She said, "Why, Frank Jefferson, don't you recognize me? I was Joyce Rollins. I married a man from out of state."

Frank felt his heart sink a little because Joy had really caught his attention. She was so pleasant and she could make that piano talk. Frank said, "Is your husband a member here? I don't think I've met him."

Joy said, "No, my husband died from a heart attack about two years after we married."

Frank quickly told her he was sorry.

She smiled and said, "It was a very happy two years together. I have nothing but good memories."

Frank thought to himself, *I wish all my memories were good.*

After that Sunday, Frank sat a little closer to the piano. He also found a seat beside Joy at the church fellowship meals.

He grew very fond of Joy, and secretly she was growing fond of Frank. She had heard how his wife had left him and the boys so suddenly and without warning. But she never pried into the matter. It was none of her business.

A Day in Court

It was the first time Marie had been back in the state of Indiana since the day she left. She was so glad that Laura Sloan was with her. After the court proceedings, they would stay overnight and start the trip back to Kansas in the morning.

Marie, along with Laura, walked into the beautiful old courthouse with mixed emotions. Marie had only been in that building a couple of times in her life.

The first time was as a teenager, when she had pled guilty to a speeding ticket and paid the fine. The second time was also as a teenager, when Frank had purchased their marriage license.

The ancient building was as she remembered it. The marble floors and stone walls still echoed with each footfall. It sounded so foreboding to her and seemed to echo even more on this day. Marie and

Laura climbed aboard the cage-like, open elevator, and the gate shut, sounding almost like a cell door closing. The elevator made a metallic, clacking sound in its assent to the second level.

In the courtroom, a stern-looking judge shuffled through some papers. Attorneys dug through their briefcases, going to and from a small, back room. The clerk of court wrote something on a small piece of paper and handed it to the bailiff, who quickly handed the paper to a deputy. Hushed voices filled the room.

Looking around, Marie spied Frank. He had his normal summer tan and he, too, had a serious, somewhat haggard look on his face. She avoided eye contact and hoped he would not contest the divorce. The last thing she wanted was a fight.

Finally, after hearing a couple of other cases, the judge peered over his reading glasses as if looking for someone in particular. He asked if Marie Holly Jefferson was present.

Marie timidly replied, "Yes, Your Honor."

He then asked if Frank Jefferson was in court. Frank held up his hand and said in a barely audible voice, "Present, Your Honor."

The judge made a few legal-sounding remarks about divorce, which Marie really did not understand. However, in the end, all she had to do was state that she and Frank had been separated for at least a year. She also stated she did not desire anything from Frank. Then this serious-looking judge said, "Because you left the children, you will have to have a separate proceeding to get custody of them." He added, "I do not see that you have a case for that."

At least he didn't use the word "abandonment."

The judge looked at Frank and asked if he wanted to contest the divorce. Frank simply said, "No, Your Honor." The gavel came down and that was that. An eleven-year marriage was terminated.

Frank was almost to the door when Marie caught up to him. She asked if she could see the boys.

He hesitated for a couple of seconds, pursed his lips, then said, "Okay, but don't upset them."

She also asked if he had any new pictures of them she could have. Again, Frank said "yes" — they had just sat for a family picture at the church.

Marie was surprised when he mentioned church. Frank had never set foot in a church, at least that she knew of. They had not even been married in a church building.

The meeting that evening at the farm was strained, to say the least. The boys reluctantly let

Marie hug them, and they accepted the small gifts she had brought them. But she was a stranger to them now. Within an hour, that visit was history.

Marie went to her parents' home after calling ahead first. They seemed rather cold toward her. They didn't even offer her a glass of tea, let alone a meal. None of her siblings were there, even though they knew she was coming over. Later, she called Frank's folks and they, too, were very distant with her. She seemed to be public enemy number one.

In the motel room that evening, Marie broke down and cried while Laura rubbed her back, stroked her hair, and tried in vain to comfort her. She did not look for a sunset that evening. The pain in her heart was too much.

The Kiss

Back in Kansas, the daily routine was pretty much the same for Marie. It was ten hours at the café, home for a sandwich in the evening, and then a short walk to the park, where she sat on a bench and watched the sunset.

One evening in late October, though it was cold, Marie was still determined to see her sunset. As she set out for the park, Brock came out of his house and asked if he could join her. She hated to refuse him, even though she felt the sunset belonged just to her. He had a thermos of coffee and a couple of Styrofoam cups in a bag. They walked briskly to the park and found her favorite bench.

The sun had not reached the horizon, so Brock opened the bag and produced the cups and two donuts. They drank the coffee and ate the donuts without saying much. As the sun set, Marie noted that it seemed so much more beautiful than it had in weeks. Perhaps it was the company.

The couple walked the long way around the park and headed home. At Marie's door, Brock took her key and unlocked her door for her. He then, without warning, cupped her chin in his hand and kissed her ever so lightly on the lips. It was not a passionate kiss, but it was so sweet. She returned the favor.

They both blushed a little, and Brock said, "I have no idea why I did that. If I have offended you, I am sorry."

"No offense taken, Brock," she replied, her lips curving into a smile. It had been a long time since she had been kissed. *Over a year,* she thought, *and never have I been kissed like that.* It was a kiss that said, "I care for you very much."

Conversions

Back in Indiana, Frank and Joy never missed a function at the church, and they usually attended together. Sometimes the boys sat between them. At other times, there were special programs just for children.

One Sunday after the morning service, Joy asked Frank if he and the boys would join her at her house for lunch. She said she had not gone to much trouble, but it was more than she could eat by herself. Frank accepted the invitation but added, "My boys can eat a lot."

It was much more than a lunch. Joy had baked a chicken and served up some old-fashioned homemade noodles, mashed potatoes, string beans, and chocolate pie. Just a very nice Hoosier Sunday dinner. Frank knew she had planned this meal just for his brood.

After dinner, he helped her with the dishes while the boys played a board game. She then asked him to sit at the kitchen table with her; she had a question for him.

"Frank, are you a Christian?"

He was a little surprised and stumbled on his words. "I . . . I think so. I try to be a good person."

"I know you're a good man, Frank. But that's not what I asked. What I mean is . . . have you ever committed your life to Christ?"

Joy spent the next twenty minutes explaining what she meant. Then she asked, "Frank would you let Jack come over and talk with you about what you need to do?"

Now, Frank wanted to please Joy, so he quickly, without thinking, said, "Sure, I would like that."

So she made a phone call to Jack right then and there. The meeting would take place at seven the next evening.

***

Now, Jack was a good preacher, but he was even better at speaking with a person one on one. He brought his Bible and asked Frank to get his Bible, which was a new one—Frank had never owned a

Bible until recently. Some of the pages in Frank's new Bible were still stuck together. But Jack was patient, and as they turned to scripture after scripture, Frank became convinced that he needed to make a commitment to Christ.

That was on Monday night. Frank and the boys went to the Wednesday night Bible study and prayer meeting. This group was smaller than the Sunday morning and Sunday night crowds. It was also more informal.

At the end of the service, an invitation was given for anyone who wanted to make a new commitment to Christ or who just wanted to give a testimony.

Frank could not help himself. He stepped out and walked the ten feet to where Jack stood. He said, "Preacher, I want to do what you told me about Monday night."

Jack hugged Frank and took his confession of faith. Frank said it boldly because he believed it. "I believe that Jesus is the Christ the son of the living God." He then went to the small dressing room next to the baptistery and dressed in a white baptismal robe. Jack and Frank stepped down into the water of the baptistery. There, Frank was immersed into Christ in the name of the Father, the Son, and the Holy Spirit.

Frank had never felt such relief and release in his life. Jack hugged him again as he came up out of the water. However, the first person Frank looked for was Joy. She had a smile on her face that stretched from ear to ear, and she winked at him.

The church members then joined in the congratulations. They offered him encouragement and support. It was a wonderful time. They all went into the fellowship hall for some refreshments that someone had mysteriously produced from somewhere.

Frank Jefferson began his new life that night. He now understood what Jesus said in the gospel of John. Jesus told Nicodemus, "You must be born again of the water and the spirit." Frank felt truly born again.

From that night on, Frank and Joy were a couple. Joy had no children of her own, but she was so good with the boys. Mike was just a little rebellious at first, but Murray and Matt immediately relished the attention she showered on them.

Joy lived comfortably, as she had received a generous insurance settlement, which she had invested and used wisely. She also taught piano to several students. Frank plodded along at the research center. It did not pay a great salary, but it was steady work. His hobby, the farm, cost him more than it produced in money. But it was a good life for the boys.

Life was good for Frank those days. As Jack often said from the pulpit: "God is good," and the people always responded, "All the time."

***

After the kiss that evening in Kansas City, Brock and Marie began to spend more time together. They sometimes watched TV, sometimes just sat and talked. Even though Marie was faithful to attend on the Sundays she didn't have to work, Brock noticed that she never partook of Communion. He thought to himself that he would ask her about this very soon.

One Sunday morning at the invitation time, Marie walked forward. Brock met her with open arms. She whispered in his ear that she wanted to say something. As the music stopped, she choked back her tears. In a broken voice she said, "I need to tell you all something about myself before I do anything else."

Marie stood in front of this small congregation and told them all about her life. How unhappy she had been for most of it. But how the last year had turned her life around. This turnaround and the new joy she had found was mainly due to Brock and this little flock of believers.

She told them she was ashamed for leaving her husband and children. But she was begging God and the people she had hurt to forgive her. Marie hoped these Christians in this little church would not hold harsh feelings toward her. Then she said, "I have come to believe in Jesus Christ and that he died to take away my sins."

She then turned her face to Brock and said, "I want you to baptize me into Christ so that my sins may be removed."

Brock had tears in his eyes as he looked out on his flock. He could see they, too, were moved with emotion. There was nothing but love and forgiveness in the faces of these Christians who had also been redeemed.

That afternoon in a large sister church across town, Marie was immersed into Christ. Almost all of that little congregation had gathered to give her the support she so badly needed. When Brock lifted her from the water, a huge burden was lifted from her heart.

In one of his sermons a few weeks before, Brock

had spoken of making restitution to those you have wronged. Marie knew she could never make restitution to Frank and her boys. She simply left this in the hands of her great God.

The Epistle

However, Marie could not get the thought of restitution off her mind. One evening she sat at the kitchen table with a lined notepad and began to write.

Dear Frank, Mike, Murray, and Matt,
I am writing this to beg your forgiveness . . .

Marie wrote two full pages filled with apologies and begged to be forgiven. She told her boys she expected great things from them and encouraged them to obey their daddy. She addressed each of the boys individually with a very private message. Marie wished Frank the best in his life and wanted her boys to be happy. She hoped Frank would find someone who would love him, as she never could. Her only request was that he would send pictures of the boys from time to time and reports of how they were doing. She said she would not bother him again, and gave him the address of the café where he could send pictures.

She told herself maybe one day she would send him a new address. When she moved on . . . *toward her sunset.*

However, Marie soon stopped going to the park to look at her sunset. She had found what she was looking for. She found contentment in a man who loved her and in the God to whom she had been led.

***

Frank honored Marie's request. He sent small school pictures of the boys faithfully every year until they each graduated. He saw no point in reports on them. The pictures told the story; they were growing up and becoming fine, handsome young men.

One by one, all three of the Jefferson boys married and began families of their own.

The Afterglow

In June of 1969, Frank Jefferson married Joyce Rollins Silvers in the Cedar Grove Christian Church. His boys all stood up with him and seemed so happy with their new mother.

They moved into Joy's home, but Frank kept the farm so that he and the boys could raise some animals, plant crops, and tend a garden.

Frank sometimes found himself in the evening out at the farm enjoying a beautiful sunset. He thought it odd. He had never noticed the sunsets before.

***

In May 1970, Marie Holly Jefferson became Mrs. Brock Weston. They were married in the little, white-frame church building by a friend from the seminary who served a large church just outside of Kansas City.

In June the following year, Marie and Brock became the parents of a seven-pound girl with curly, black hair and blue-green eyes whom they named Faith. The wonderful man who had rescued her had also given her this beautiful child.

Marie silently thanked God that she did not have to suffer forever because of sins and mistakes in her past. She also realized she had found something in God's creation *far more precious than a sunset.*

***

The Jefferson Boys
Shortly after he graduated from high school, Matt Jefferson went off by himself to Canada, camping and hiking. He was still the independent one. He then returned home, bought an over-the-road truck, and started hauling produce all over the Midwest. He met a beautiful young woman named Janet at a grocery store in Iowa, where she worked. Something about her reminded him of his mother. At least, the way he remembered her.

They courted for about six months every time Matt was in town. One day, Matt showed up at the grocery store. He got down on one knee right there in the produce department, in front of complete strangers, and asked Janet if she would marry him. When she said "yes," the strangers in the store cheered.

After being married by a justice of the peace, they honeymooned from the cab of his truck all the way back to Indiana. Frank and Joy were shocked but pleased when Matt showed up with a new bride from Iowa. Within a couple of years, Matt and Janet had a beautiful daughter, whom they named Frances Marie.

***

Mike Jefferson was a good student in school. He graduated and was the salutatorian of his senior class. He graduated from Purdue University with a degree in agriculture. With a little political pull from his dad, Mike attained a position as the county agriculture extension agent. He then fell head over heels in love and married Doris Ramsey, whom he had known since grade school, and they had twin boys. These two boys became Papaw Frank's constant companions when he went out to the farm.

***

Murray Jefferson went to school at Indiana

University. It was quite a time, with much bantering and teasing in the Jefferson family when the Purdue graduate and the IU graduate got together, especially at basketball tournament time.

Murray got his MD degree, but instead of practicing medicine, he went to work at Eli Lilly and Company, the research center where Frank had worked years before. He married Samantha, a nurse he had met in medical school. She had lived all her life in Bloomington; however, she quickly adjusted to country life and promptly quit nursing when she became pregnant. Four children came along in quick succession, each a little less than two years apart. Samantha stayed home and raised the two boys and two girls. They were a tightly knit family. There was always joking, storytelling, and a loving atmosphere at the dinner table.

***

All three of the Jefferson boys had made a vow to live close to their roots. They kept that vow and lived within a few miles of where they were raised.

Murray and Mike built homes within shouting distance of Frank's little farm. These two families, along with Frank and Joy, all worshipped at Cedar

Grove Christian Church. They often ate Sunday dinner together after church. Those were happy times.

Matt, always the independent one, built a home about fifteen miles away in the city. He and Janet worshipped with a small, struggling congregation, one where Matt said he could actually "do some good." There, he taught several boys in an "all boys" Sunday school class. These boys were from a rough part of town. They were mostly from broken, single-parent homes. But Matt had a way with them, and he actually did "do some good." He made a tangible difference in their lives. He and Janet often took two or three boys home with them on Sunday for an afternoon of basketball, fishing, or just hanging out.

The Tradition

Frank insisted that the Jefferson family should start a tradition. He said traditions kept families together. Frank maintained the old farmhouse well. He kept the electricity on and kept the yard mowed. Each summer in July, Frank, Joyce, the boys, and their families all met at the old Jefferson home for a reunion.

They would gather for at least three days. They brought tents, air mattresses, and grills. They picnicked, cooked out, played badminton, pitched horseshoes, and played basketball under the old hoop fastened to the barn.

At night, they played cards or a board game until after midnight. The rules were that they could not make or receive any phone calls unless it was an emergency. This was family time.

They shared and made wonderful memories at

the old homeplace. It was a time for refreshing themselves. They reminisced and relived their childhoods.

The best part of this tradition took place on the last evening before they were to leave and go home. The children were to gather enough wood to build a bonfire.

As the sun was about to set below the hill, they made a circle around the fire. All fifteen of them joined hands as Frank lifted a prayer for his family. He thanked the Lord they were so blessed to know Jesus. He thanked the Lord this circle was unbroken: they were all alive and healthy.

Eventually, the last ember stopped glowing, and there was only a small wisp of smoke, like a lingering prayer rising to heaven.

Epilogue

The Last Sunset

Three handsome men, along with their families, escorted a lonely casket up a low hill on a little farm in Indiana. A few generic words of comfort were spoken by the young preacher from the Cedar Grove Christian Church. He was new to the church and had not known the man in the casket very long.

The coffin was lowered, and the family stepped to the side to greet several people who had come to pay their last respects to Frank Jefferson. There was a gravestone with two names on it. Half of the headstone read:

Joyce Rollins Jefferson
Born July 23, 1936 - died Oct. 16, 2010

And on the other side was chiseled:

Frank Jefferson
Born May 3, 1936 - died ----

Down the hill stood an older man and woman who seemed to be just looking on—visitors to the funeral. They did not appear to be grieving. The woman finally made her way to the three men and hugged each one of them without saying a word. She and the man then slowly walked to the foot of the hill, turned, and watched the sun as it winked one last time and was gone.

If the three men recognized the woman, they never let on.

***

Once in the car on their way back to Kansas, Marie leaned over and hugged Brock's arm. "Thank you, Brock, for bringing me back to say goodbye to my boys. I never loved their father as a husband, but I never stopped thinking about my boys. I never stopped loving them."

Brock smiled at Marie, squeezed her hand, and began to sing in his beautiful baritone voice—a song she loved to hear him sing. *"Beyond the sunset no clouds will gather. No storms will threaten, no fears annoy . . ."*

About the Author

Phil Emmert began his second career when he left a secure job with the Dow Chemical Company in Indiana, where he was a research assistant. At age thirty-three, he sold his little farm near Lebanon, Indiana, and enrolled in Johnson Bible College near Knoxville, Tennessee. Upon his graduation, he went into the full-time ministry, preaching in several different Christian churches and Churches of Christ.

Phil has worn many hats in his seventy-eight years. He has been an animal technician, part time farmer, research assistant, school bus driver, substitute schoolteacher, children's social worker, and a juvenile crime prevention counselor in a county school system. All the while, he was ministering to small churches in Tennessee and North Carolina.

From all his experiences with people and especially with children, Phil became aware that young people are ignorant of American history. Therefore, at the age of seventy-seven, he began his third career: published author. He penned the WWII-era books *When War Was Heck* and *The Afterglow of War: Lessons Learned*.

Phil is the father of four adult children, about which he says, *"They are my greatest accomplishments."* He has eleven grandchildren. He also has three adult stepchildren.